# A Pony IN THE FIELD

Other Apple Paperbacks
you will enjoy:

*Summer Stories* by Nola Thacker

*A Cry in the Night* by Carol Ellis

*The Latchkey Kids* by Carol Stanley

*Thirteen* by Candice Ransom

*Kate's House* by Mary Francis Shura

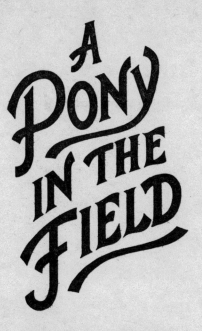

# A PONY IN THE FIELD

## MARION DOREN

AN
**APPLE**
PAPERBACK

SCHOLASTIC INC.
New York Toronto London Auckland Sydney

ISBN 0-590-43663-5

Copyright © 1991 by Marion Doren.
All rights reserved.
Published by Scholastic Inc.
APPLE PAPERBACKS is a registered trademark of
Scholastic Inc.

12 11 10 9 8 7 6 5 4 3 2 1          1 2 3 4 5 6/9

Printed in the U.S.A.                    28

First Scholastic printing, March 1991

# 1

**M**eg Kirtland stepped away from the shadow of the shed and into the hot summer sun. Fifth grade had ended at noon. Now that summer was here, what was she going to do with it?

Green grass struggled through last year's dead stalks. What this field needed was a horse. What Meg needed was a horse. She pretended there was a horse down by the stream, hidden by the slender trees bunched there. She stalked the horse like an Indian, noiseless feet pressing down the grass, moving quietly by the rusting old bathtub where McLaughlin's cows drank when the McLaughlins had owned Meadowbrook Farm; down to the stream where the blue flag iris grew. In late summer she could walk across the little brook, but now she had to walk along it, stepping from hummock to hummock.

Meg imagined the horse walking out from the spinney of trees and standing patiently until she

1

pulled herself up and galloped along the stone wall to the rise where her riding ring was going to be.

The night before, when the six Kirtlands were eating at the picnic table in the old kitchen, Meg had brought up the subject again. "A pony or a horse would keep that field cleared."

Brad snorted whenever she said horse. "What we need around here is a tractor," he had said. "A tractor could tame that field in a minute. I could mow the lawn, too." Brad was seven, and not someone to be trusted on a tractor.

Dan had had other ideas. "Chickens are better. There's already a chicken coop out there. I could feed them and sell the eggs." Dan was a year younger than Brad, and neither of them ever wanted the same things Meg wanted.

Meg had shaken her head. "I don't think you can have chickens in a horse field." She needed someone on her side, but year-old Kara just sat in her high chair and smiled, not choosing a horse or a tractor or chickens.

Meg turned from the trees and tossed her hair: a palomino mane, she had decided after reading one of her horse books, a mane pale and straight, often falling down over her eyes. Her mother kept insisting that Meg let her cut the straggles, but Meg refused, hoping her hair would grow long enough to put into a ponytail. She had never seen a live palomino, but guessed that its eyes wouldn't be the same blue-green as hers and that its light coat wouldn't freckle like her nose did.

Meg slapped her legs into a gallop. Outcroppings of granite stuck up from the ground and she had to watch her step. The McLaughlins had sold the farm to Meg's family a year before and moved to Florida. Generations of people had tried to farm this rocky land without much success, but it was a perfect place for horses.

When Meg reached the rise where her horse ring would be, she slowed to a walk and went around a circle she had traced every day since the snow had melted. Hooves would wear a better path than sneakers, but she put herself through her paces anyway. By the end of summer she would have worn a practice ring down.

Brad waved to her from the gate. "Mom wants you. She's got to go back to school and finish cleaning her classroom."

Meg dropped her imaginary reins. So much for summer vacation. She wished her mother would quit teaching school and stay home, but if she did that there would be no chance of a horse or a tractor.

"Sorry, Meg," her mother said. "I'll only be a couple of hours. Why don't you take Kara for a walk? Your father should be home at four, so I trust the boys will be all right until then."

Meg cleaned Kara's face and brushed her baby curls, then smoothed her own palomino mane. The old McLaughlin farm was at the end of the road, so there was only one way to go — toward civilization. She plopped Kara in a stroller and walked slowly and quietly down the street, not to stalk a horse, but to escape before Brad and Dan saw her going.

Too late. The boys were sending twigs down the stream where it flowed under the road. They dropped them on one side, then raced to the other side to watch them come out. Now the boys buzzed around the stroller making engine sounds. Meg wondered why her brothers liked motors instead of horses. Anyone with brains knew horses were better, and that was probably the boys' trouble. Her mother drove away in the van. She was smiling because she knew Meg would take care of everyone.

Clouds of gnats hung around Kara's face and tried to fly up Meg's nose, so she pushed the stroller with one hand and waved the other hand at the bugs. She was so busy she almost bumped into a blue moving van in front of the old Bott's farm. All the farms were named for their previous owners, so Meg lived in the old McLaughlin place, and for the year she'd lived there, the Bott farm had stood empty. She stopped the stroller to watch two men carry a large bed in the open front door. Brad and Dan leaped into the van before Meg could tell them not to. She knew they wouldn't listen, but she yelled for them to come out, anyway.

A dark-haired woman and a little girl of about three walked out of the house. "Hi, blondie," the woman said, kneeling by Kara's stroller. "I'm Mrs. Madison. Do you live around here?" She talked to Kara, but Meg knew the question was for her.

"We're the Kirtlands. I'm Meg, this is Kara, and the two monsters in the van are Dan and Brad. We live up the street. Our parents are Janet and Bill Kirtland."

The little girl swung shyly around her mother's skirt. "I'm Tina," she said. "I'm three."

"It's good to know someone else lives on this road. Tell your mother we'll be up as soon as we're settled." Mrs. Madison stood up. "We're in a mess right now, but come to the door anyway. Sam would love to meet you."

Sam. Meg's heart dipped. A boy. There were too many boys around here already. She watched Brad and Dan run down the van ramp. "No, that's all right. I'll meet him another time."

Tina giggled. Mrs. Madison called up to an open window. "Sam, come on down. There's someone you'll want to meet."

Meg pushed the stroller to the door. There was

5

a clattering on the narrow stairs and a pair of long legs appeared, followed by shorts, a shirt, and a face framed by long, dark hair. Meg blinked, surprised at seeing a girl her own age. She examined Sam, her straight nose, the smile showing teeth a little too big for the firm mouth, her skin tanned, without a hint of freckles.

"Samantha, this is Meg, and her sister, Kara."

Samantha stuck out a grimy hand. "Hi. If I'd known there would be a girl nearby, I wouldn't have made such a fuss about moving. You're the best thing that's happened since we left Nova Scotia," she said.

Meg classified Sam as a thoroughbred, lean and muscled, while Meg was more like a Welsh pony, with broader shoulders and shorter legs. She took Samantha's hand and pulled her outside. She wanted to say Sam was the best thing to happen to her since she was born, but the words stuck in her throat. The Kirtlands didn't say mushy things, no matter how comfortable and loving her family was.

"She thought you were a boy," Tina said to Sam. "Where's someone to be my friend? I can't play with them." She pointed at Brad and Dan running round and round the blue van.

"Wait awhile. Kara will grow up soon. Come meet the boys," Meg said. Samantha helped her push the stroller across the grass. They reached the street, and the boys screeched to a stop. "This is Sam," Meg said.

Brad snorted. "You call that a Sam?" He and Dan gagged, grabbing their middles to show how disgusting girls were.

Meg, Tina, and Sam laughed, and even Kara smiled. Brad and Dan revved up their engines and roared back toward home.

# 2

The McLaughlins had named their farm Meadowbrook Farm, and a faded wooden sign with MEADOWBROOK FARM lettered in blue paint hung above the barn door. Meg showed Sam the barn first when she visited the next day. It was a kind of test, but Meg couldn't help herself. As much as she needed a friend, she needed someone who liked the same things she did. If Sam were a thoroughbred, she would want to see the barn before she had a tour of the farmhouse.

Meg slid the massive door open and stood with her new friend as their eyes adjusted to the light. The inside of the barn smelled of musty hay, the air speckled with the dust of a century, motes dancing in the dim sunlight that crept in through broken windows. There were twelve stalls, each with an old-fashioned name over it: *Blossom, Daisy, Rose.* Meg guided Sam over holes in the floor, testing the floorboards as she went.

"You have enough to look at for another hundred years," Sam marveled.

"I've spent a year looking it over, but I never had anyone to show it to before. The boys run around like windup toys, breaking anything they find. And it's too dangerous for Kara."

The hayloft stretched across the back of the barn, but in the front Meg and Sam could look straight up to the beams and trusses, and the cupola on top. At the back of each stanchion was a trapdoor where the manure was shoveled down to the dirt floor below.

"Mom says there's a fortune in dried manure down there," Meg said. "She uses it for her vegetable garden."

Sam peered down. "Three stories. Wouldn't it make a wonderful house? Put big windows over there, and sit at dinner and look out on the fields and those pine trees. Oh, it would be perfect."

"You haven't seen anything yet." Meg was so pleased with Sam's reaction, she had to keep herself from doing something foolish, like cartwheeling or singing. She had to act like an almost-fifth-grader or Sam might think she was too young and silly. "Come out and I'll show you the rest of the buildings."

Stepping out of the barn was like walking out of an afternoon movie into the bright sunshine. A low, white building at the western side of the barn was the spring house. It smelled damp and clean. Meg removed the whitewashed board covering the spring.

"I don't see anything," Sam said.

"Me neither. But I dropped a pebble down once and heard it splash. A long way down. Kara isn't allowed in here, and you have to keep Tina out. Everyone has town water now so the spring isn't used anymore."

Next to the spring house stood a small structure containing an old circular saw. "The McLaughlins cut wood here in the winter and piled it on the street to sell. One of their grandsons still lives in town and he tells me stories about them. He has pictures of old Ben McLaughlin doing farmwork in a three-piece suit. No overalls for him."

A huge spiderweb in the glassless window persuaded them they'd rather be outside. In back of the barn was a two-story shed with rusting tools in sad heaps. Behind that the silo tilted, half its siding gone.

Between the house and the barn was a circular driveway with the open carriage house connecting to the back of the house. Next to the carriage house was a two-story building. "Enter my secret hideaway," Meg said, opening the door. "That big machine is a cranberry sorter. Townspeople came to the bogs to pick. There's an old picture of them, mostly women wearing sunbonnets, babies strapped to their backs. I'll show you the bogs someday."

The back room had an old potbellied stove in one corner, and a workbench with blackened tools strewn on it, as if old Ben McLaughlin had left them one day and never came back.

A door made from a packing case with PROVIDENCE, R.I., printed on it, led to the second floor, where old boxes and the legs of a table lay on the floor. Beneath the only window, the feathers of a pigeon clustered on fragile bones.

Sam shuddered. "It's a graveyard. I like the downstairs better."

They went single file down the narrow staircase, raced through the back room, out the back door, and into the field.

"They left everything, didn't they?" Sam said when she saw the bathtub.

"McLaughlin's cows drank out of that. I'll fill it up when I get my horse." Meg giggled nervously, afraid to look at Sam. If Sam didn't love horses as much as Meg did, what would they have in common?

"Your horse?" Samantha sat on a large, warm rock. "What horse?"

Meg joined her. "Wild roses grow over this rock. Watch out for the prickers. *My* horse. The one I'm going to get someday. This will be its field. That's its bathtub."

11

Sam tossed back her hair and raised her face to the sun. "I can just see your horse galloping around the field. When's it coming? Will you teach me how to ride?"

A warmth flooded through Meg. Finally a real friend who hadn't laughed at her when she shared her dream. She spread her arms out to capture her field with its invisible horse. "I wish it would come tomorrow, but I'm afraid we have a long wait. Right now all I can do is wish on the first star and when I see a load of hay."

"I love it all, even without the horse. Nova Scotia was pretty, but it was so far from everything. Cold, too, though I guess it can get cold here." Sam, her dark eyes flecked with gold, looked straight at Meg. "You must be rich to own all this."

"Afraid not. Mom and Dad teach school. Mom went back to teaching when they bought the farm. Most all of this," she waved her arm to include several coops and a matted grid of fallen chicken wire tangled in the grass, "is not in very good shape. We moved here because we needed more room when Kara was born."

"When do you think you'll get your horse?"

"Someday," Meg said airily, uncoiling from the rock. "C'mon, I'll show you the house."

Meg led Sam into the house through a back door off the carriage house. The hallway was lined with trash bags ready for the dump, and a line of hooks held jackets and hats.

In the large kitchen, the sink, stove, and refrigerator stood apart from each other. There were no cabinets or countertops, and dishes sat on a bookcase against the wall. Meg's mother was mixing something in a bowl, her eyes on a book propped against the wall. She wore shorts and a T-shirt and old, faded sneakers. Her brown hair curled lightly on her neck. Kara walked back and forth, holding onto the bench of the picnic table.

"Mom, this is Sam. You know. Sam Madison. I told you they moved into the Bott's place. Sam's mother will come up to see you when she's settled."

"Hi, Sam," Mom waved the mixing spoon. "Welcome to Elm Street. Meg's been needing someone her own age around here. I wish I could think of something besides tuna salad for lunch."

"You don't need a recipe for that, do you, Mom?"

"Oh, heavens, no. This is one of the library books I picked up yesterday. There's no time to read during the school year, so I end up reading and stirring mayonnaise and keeping an eye on Kara during summer vacation."

Meg pulled Sam along. She showed her the pantry behind the kitchen where the McLaughlins used to separate the milk, and the room over the kitchen where there were more odds and ends of furniture. "The McLaughlins used to sleep up here when the kitchen was the whole house. It's not heated. They say the boys used to get up on winter mornings and run outside to warm their feet in fresh cow flaps." Meg giggled.

"Cow flaps?"

"You know. Manure. I just hope they washed their feet before they went to school."

Meg hurried Sam through the large, haphazard downstairs. "This is the funeral room. It has no heat. Old Ben built this while his wife was dying upstairs. I wonder how she felt, hearing him hammer away."

She waved at her parents' bedroom. "Probably was the front parlor. See? Dad made a closet. The bathroom's in there."

Upstairs they passed the boys' room, Kara's small bedroom and, as she led Sam around the stairwell, Meg felt the usual dizzy feeling. The floor tilted so that she felt she was heading over the banister.

"And this is my room."

She heard Sam let out a deep breath. "I do not believe it."

Meg laughed. "Neither could my parents. We moved here last spring, and the room was pretty shabby. When Mom asked me what I wanted for my birthday, I said a horse, and when she said

14

no, I said paint for my bedroom. I chose the colors and did most of the painting, at least down low. Dad did the rest. Mom said it gives her a headache and she won't come in here."

Sam danced into the room and turned around several times. "It's wonderful. Only I feel like saluting, or singing 'The Star-Spangled Banner.' Let me guess. Your birthday must be on the Fourth of July."

"How'd you guess? I've always loved those colors. These are not quite flag colors. The red has some blue in it, so it doesn't look like blood."

The east and west walls were blue, and the north and south red. The blue walls had red trim on the window ledges and door moldings, and the red walls had blue. White curtains hung at the windows, and the bedspread was blue with white stars.

"Magic. That's what it is. Pure magic."

Meg showed her the letters in the plaster over the inside of the closet door: *Plastered by Ben McLaughlin 1855.* "That's the old Ben I think was so interesting. He had a son, Ben Jr., and another son, John. We bought the farm from Daniel of the next generation, I think."

Sam examined the horse books, the horse sketches Meg had drawn, and the line of model horses across the mantel of the closed-off fireplace.

"I would know whose room this was even if you hadn't told me."

"You haven't seen the attic or the cellar. Then we'll have tuna sandwiches." Meg scrabbled through her mind for all the places to show Sam. Why, with this old farmhouse it would take days.

"Let's see the attic first. We're already up two flights. Is this the door out here in the hall?" Sam had her hand on the knob, just about to pull the door open.

"Meg," her mother's voice called up the stairs, "Mrs. Madison is on the phone sounding a little hysterical. Seems she's lost a daughter."

"Tell her I've got more to see," Sam yelled down.

"And tell her you'll give Sam lunch," Meg added.

"Tell her I'll be back by dark," Sam said.

"I think you'll have to come down and tell her yourself." They could hear Meg's mother walk back to the phone in the kitchen.

"I'll talk her into letting me stay," Sam said over her shoulder, as she ran down the stairs. In the kitchen, she took the receiver and said breathlessly, "Hi, Mother, I'm fine, don't worry about me, we just haven't finished seeing everything. Mrs. Kirtland will let me stay for lunch. Won't you?" She gave a pleading look.

Meg's mother nodded.

"What? Oh, not now. Couldn't you go choose wallpaper some other time? This is really important." Sam listened for a few moments. "Yes, I know I said I'd be right back, but it's only been a little while." She listened some more, casting her eyes down. "Yes. I know. I'll be right there." She hung up the phone.

"I have to feed Tina her lunch. I guess I have to go."

Meg had hoped, but hoping wasn't enough. Wallpaper was important to a grown-up. The joy went out of the morning. "I'll walk you to the door."

"Thanks, Mrs. Kirtland, for inviting me. I'll eat lunch here some other time." Sam led the way down the hall.

She left by the front door with its etched glass and the iron doorbell that you cranked like a coffee grinder. When the door closed behind Sam, the hall felt cooler. It was not cooler because the sun was shut out, but because Sam had gone. How had Meg ever lived without Sam? Suddenly lonely, Meg ran to the kitchen, where her mother and Kara and the tuna fish sandwiches were. It was no time to be alone.

# 3

Meg woke early and padded barefoot on the warm floor. Sunlight flooded into the room through the two eastern windows. She shaded her eyes and tried to see through the pear trees down to Sam's house, but the green leaves hung thickly now that the blossoms had dropped. Sam. A friend. Meg almost forgot to change the positions of her horses. Every day she faced them a different way so they would work their magic and draw a horse to her house. Quickly she turned them toward Sam's house before she smoothed her bed. If a horse did not come up the road, maybe Sam would.

Meg dressed quickly and gathered yesterday's clothes for the downstairs hamper. She had the neatest spot in the whole house because her mother refused to set foot in the red-and-blue room. Meg's mother tried to keep the house clean, but what with four children, a classroom, and

18

this big old house, she went off in all directions.

Meg turned once again to the east window, thinking how perfectly wonderful it was that Sam lived just beyond the pear trees and was probably getting ready for breakfast at this very moment, too. She tried to imagine living in a neat house with a mother who stayed home and a sister who didn't pester anyone and with no brothers at all.

Early as she was, the other two bedrooms upstairs were empty. The boys had to be pulled out of their beds on school days, but vacations were different. Kara's room was small, with nothing much in it but a crib and a dresser. The boys' room had bunk beds with clothes draped over them. Two bookcases held Brad's books, because whenever he sat still, he read. Dan's shelves were covered with models in various stages of construction: cars, ships, and airplanes. For as much as the boys looked alike, with close-cropped hair and brown eyes, they were different. As Meg went down the stairs she thought about how strange it was that Brad, the reader, liked tractors, and Dan, the model-maker, preferred chickens.

Everyone was in the kitchen except Meg's father, who loved to sleep late and rarely had the chance. Physical education instructors worked a year-round schedule, with sports in the summer as well as during the school term. Her mother stood at the stove, sipping coffee and reading.

Kara sat in her high chair, eating cold cereal. Brad walked around, shedding toast crumbs, while Dan held the refrigerator door open as he checked on the cluttered contents. As soon as Kara was older she would not be sitting down either, since breakfast was always a make-it-yourself meal, and the family sat at the table only at dinnertime.

It was like a silent movie with everyone busily eating and no one talking. Meg took an apple and a muffin, and almost got out the door.

"Who's the apple for? Your horse?" Brad said.

Brothers should be locked up until they are old enough to vote, Meg decided. "Yup," she answered, taking a chunk out of the apple as she ran outside to gallop around the field.

Sam ran up the road after lunch and Meg, who had kept an eye out for her all morning, met her where the stream crossed under the street. "I was hoping you'd come," Meg said, feeling strangely shy.

"I said I would. I never lived so close to anyone before. Especially someone my age. I'm so glad you're a girl."

"I know. When your mother called 'Sam,' I was so disappointed. Mom says I'll like boys later, but right now all I've got is the Terribles, Dan and Brad. Come on." Meg reached out a hand and felt

Sam's fingers squeeze hers. "Let's go up to the attic. We didn't get up there yesterday."

The door to the attic was next to Meg's bedroom door. Meg tugged it open and pulled a string to light the bulb hanging over the narrow staircase. "I don't like to go up alone. There's no railing around the stairs, so watch your step."

Sam followed Meg and examined the two attic rooms and a large cedar closet full of old pictures and frames. "It's like they only left for a little while and are coming back soon," Sam said with a shiver, in spite of the summer heat.

"Maybe the McLaughlins'll come back today," Meg said in a low, ghostly voice. They giggled.

"My mother and I talked about my room when I got back yesterday," Sam said as they sat on the floor near the back window. "She thinks an old house should look like an old house, cluttered with things hanging on the walls, like baskets and wooden spoons. I had to choose paint and wallpaper from some samples she had. Guess I'm not ready for red, white, and blue, anyway. Want to help me when the stuff comes?"

"Sure," Meg said. "I can paint as high as I can reach, but I haven't tried wallpaper."

"My mother'll do that. We have to paint first. Want to do it tomorrow? She's going to the paint store this afternoon."

"Can't. Tomorrow's Saturday."

They watched bluebottle flies batting at the window. "Can we let them out?" Sam asked.

They wrestled with the old window. "This is the only window in the whole house that faces north. Those McLaughlins were smart. The winter wind rattles this one till it sounds like it's going to fall out." They finally got the window open a crack, probably the first time in fifty years, and coaxed the flies out with an old newspaper.

The field stretched out below them, and Meg was sure she could see her riding ring. Her sneakers had made a mark on the field.

"Why can't you paint tomorrow? Saturday's the same as any other day when there's no school," Sam said.

"Seems my family can't get out of the habit. We all go to school in the winter, and Saturday's the only day we have to do our things."

"What things?"

"Mom drops us off. Brad takes a trumpet lesson at school, and I have a riding lesson at High Ridge Stables. That's on the other side of town, near Middleford. Dan and Kara go food shopping with Mom."

"What does your father do?"

Meg shrugged. "Whatever. He's coaching a baseball team, and next month he'll start football practice. Tomorrow he's going fishing. Now I want you to see the cellar."

The girls went down the three flights of stairs, through a dark hall, to the cellar door. Meg pulled the string for the lights. The floor and walls of the cellar were granite. "Mom says that's what's under her garden. Solid granite. Last year some of it heaved up and broke a Rototiller blade."

Under the sprawling house, the cellar was divided into five rooms separated by walls of whitewashed brick. Meg pointed out a signature on one wall: *Bricked by Ben Jr. 1916.*

"This is larger than our whole house," Sam said.

"It's clean and dry, but dark. Ugh. I'd hate to live underground. Let's go up."

When they burst into warm sunlight, Sam asked, "Could I watch you tomorrow?"

Meg hesitated. Often things didn't go well at High Ridge, the riding school where she took her lessons. "I guess so. Just don't expect too much."

Meg wore jeans and rubber boots with heels that looked like riding boots if you didn't get too close. The only real riding gear she had was her hard hat, and Miss Jane insisted on that.

High Ridge was run by the Browns. Miss Jane was the oldest of eight children, and she and her sister Ann did most of the teaching. Even Pop

Brown, who had a business in town, spent his weekends riding a horse, a lawn mower, or a truck. Mrs. Brown, a warm, motherly woman, often came out to stand by the fence and watch the lessons. Callie, the youngest Brown, took lessons along with Meg.

Brad and Dan sat in the way-back of the van, bothering the driver of the car behind them. While they waggled fingers and stuck out tongues, Meg worried about which horse she would get.

Chieftain, again. Chieftain was old, blind in one eye, and only dimly sighted in the other. He was slow. And unpredictable. Meg got him because the Barn Rats had first pick, and often made their choices during the week when they provided unpaid labor at the riding stable. Meg could not belong to the Barn Rats. Mothers of Barn Rats stayed every Saturday through all the classes. Barn Rats were driven over during the week to muck out stalls. Barn Rats wore proper riding clothes bought from the saddlery. Meg could never be a Barn Rat because there wasn't enough money for jodphurs and proper boots, and not enough time for her mother to drive her over after school.

All of the Barn Rats were girls, most about Meg's age. Horse lovers of high school or college age had other things to do with their time instead of cleaning stalls and saddle-soaping reins and saddles. Besides Callie, blonde and quiet, there were the snippy Lavoie sisters, Nicole and Vanessa, and the Doles, two fair-haired girls, Cathy and Doreen, whose mother rode in adult activities. Another girl who showed up regularly was Maria, dark-eyed and quick. Her mother made saddle blankets and repaired riding clothes to pay for Maria's lessons. Sporadically, boys like Ned and Larry showed up, but it was the girls who were the most devoted, sometimes even staying overnight in the barn. Others drifted in and out, depending on whether they had money for lessons, or got more involved with music lessons or ballet or whatever.

The more experienced riders had classes first, and were already in the ring where they worked on high jumps over different obstacles. Meg and others in her class did some jumping, but were not as advanced. Vanessa and Nicole Lavoie groomed Chieftain in the cross-ties.

"Chieftain's been waiting all week for you," Vanessa said. There was always a sneer in her voice. She was slim, quite attractive, and muscular. A classmate of Meg's and a horse lover, too, she could have been a good friend, but there was always that something about her that said "I'm better than you."

Nicole, Vanessa's younger sister, laughed. "We gave him a vitamin shot so he can stand up for an hour."

Meg reluctantly introduced Sam to the Lavoie sisters. Even though the Lavoies had horses and a jumping course at home, they spent much of their time at High Ridge. Their eyes brightened when they saw Sam. Meg guessed that Sam got that reaction often. No one was more special than Sam.

"Are you going to take a lesson today?" Vanessa asked.

Sam shook her head. "Today I'm going to watch Meg ride."

The sisters looked at each other with mock sadness. "Then you're not going to learn much. Chieftain is not a beast you can learn from," Vanessa said.

Although she said Sam couldn't learn anything from *Chieftain*, Meg knew she meant Sam couldn't learn anything watching *her*. But she should have expected that. Meg removed her hard hat to cool her head. If there was a meanness contest, the Lavoie sisters would win every time.

Sam pretended not to notice their unpleasantness. "Why do they give you Chieftain, Meg? He's much too big for you."

Meg shrugged. If Sam stayed around High

Ridge long enough, she'd soon see that the Barn Rats led the pecking order.

Miss Jane strode over and helped saddle and bridle Chieftain and then gave Meg a leg up. "Have a good ride," she whispered. She led Meg down to the ring, Sam following close behind to stand outside the fence.

Sometimes Chieftain followed the horse ahead of him, but today he was not interested. He switched his tail and shook his head. Meg jabbed him with her rubber boots, which did not have the same effect as spurs would have. Miss Jane gave him a swat with her crop, and he took a few steps before another standstill.

"Get a car," Vanessa said as she passed them.

First the riders had their horses walk around the ring, and Chieftain reluctantly fell into line. Meg relaxed, beginning to feel more comfortable. She nodded at Sam as they passed her.

"Everyone, trot," Miss Jane said through her megaphone.

Chieftain roused himself to trot, then stumbled, lowering his head to get his balance. Meg lost her reins and almost lost her seat. She hoped Sam hadn't seen the misstep, but when she looked up, Sam waved cheerfully.

Now Chieftain stopped dead, and the other riders passed as Meg tried to start him up again.

It was like trying to start a car without a battery, but finally Chieftain's ears twitched and he began a slow trot.

Miss Jane switched instructions from a posting trot to a sitting one and then to a trot without stirrups. Meg slipped her boots out of the stirrups, pleased that the horse was moving with the rest, when Chieftain began making very embarrassing noises. Meg's face grew hot. As they passed Sam each time, she kept her head down, hoping that the hour would soon pass.

"Canter," Miss Jane called. Meg put her boots back into the stirrups and urged her horse to stretch out his legs. He cantered twice around the ring before breaking back into a trot. Meg gave up. If she pushed him any more, he might just drop dead. She guided him to the ring opening, slowing him down to a walk. Sweat glistened on Chieftain's coat and he wheezed noisily. Thundering hooves passed them as she slid out of the saddle and led the horse out of the ring.

Meg walked Chieftain back to the barn and cooled him down before Miss Jane caught up with them. "Sorry he's such a stubborn beast. He's been a pet for so long, he's used to having his own way."

"When I get my horse, I'll ride as well as those two." Meg pointed to Vanessa and Nicole.

"Better." Miss Jane went to law school and used words carefully. "They are much too rash and would jump a horse to death if I let them."

Sam came up and helped Meg curry and brush Chieftain and put him in his stall.

Callie joined them, walking her large pony. "Tough luck today. I saw him playing his tricks. He really ought to be retired. When you get your own horse, you can bring him over to ride."

Callie was the nicest of the Barn Rats, mostly because she didn't have to prove anything. After all, her parents owned High Ridge, and Miss Jane was her sister.

"Thanks," Meg said. She knew she had opened her mouth once too often, mentioning the horse she would get some day. Now everyone believed a horse was in the near future, all because of her careless talk. The truth was that she didn't see a horse in her future at all. "Isn't there anything I can do so I can get another mount? Chieftain just isn't going to behave for me."

Callie looked at her and shook her head. "Not if you can't come over at least one day a week and muck out. We have all those mothers who'll scream if their child gets Chieftain, and they sit here every Saturday, watching to make sure the lesson is a good one. Can't your mother. . . ?"

"No," Meg said. "My mother can't."

*     *     *

Meg curled up on the backseat next to the bags of groceries, her eyes glued to the window so she didn't have to look at Sam. If Sam had thought she'd see an expert in the ring, today she learned otherwise. All Meg turned out to be was a dreamer who couldn't handle an old animal for an hour. She hoped she wouldn't lose her best friend because she couldn't manage Chieftain.

"How was it?" her mother asked.

"Fine," Meg said glumly. She felt guilty that her mother had paid for an hour's worth of her sitting on Chieftain's back while he stumbled his way around the ring.

Brad whinnied. "Sit downwind, Meg. You smell like a horse." He and Dan held their noses and made faces all the way home. Meg sniffed the horse smell on her fingers and resolved not to wash her hands all day. It was such a lovely smell.

# 4

Meg lay on her star-studded spread, rereading a Walter Farley book. Rain hit the porch roof below her window, keeping her company. Kara napped and the boys played a noisy game in front of a noisier television downstairs. Mom was somewhere reading, and Dad watched a ball game on the kitchen television.

The phone rang and four voices called, "Meg!" She never got phone calls.

It was Sam. "Want to do some painting?"

Meg put on her slicker and galloped down the road. The stream foamed merrily, but the world had a Sunday stillness, without even the sound of a bird.

Mrs. Madison met her at the door, Tina holding onto her skirt as she had the first day. "Meg. It's good to see you. Sam's upstairs, first door on your right."

Meg didn't need directions even though this was

the first time she'd visited Sam, because the strong paint smell guided her.

"I'm painting the high spots, and you work on the lower ones. There's a brush over there." Sam stood on a small ladder to paint the molding over a window.

"What color is that?" Meg asked.

"Some kind of colonial blue, though it seems more gray than blue. As long as it's colonial, my mother approves. Take a look at the wallpaper on the bed before your hands get painty."

The paper was white with small flowers the same gray-blue as the paint.

"Nice," said Meg.

"Like yesterday's lesson was fine?"

"All right. I don't like colors that are gray or muddy. I like things bright. I bet those people in the colonies liked bright paint, too. But they painted their houses so long ago that the bright colors turned to gray."

"I bet you're right. I just don't think we can make my mother believe that. Anyway, she says this won't show dirt."

Meg dipped her brush into the paint, then started carefully stroking the old woodwork. "Yesterday was not fine. I don't know why those Lavoie girls are so mean. They have horses and jumps at home, so why do they have to take over High Ridge?"

"I don't know. But I think what happened to you was terrible. Those sisters can hurt your feelings more than you can hurt mine about the paint. You care about riding and getting into that group. I don't care what color my room is, as long as it looks good."

Meg bent over the paint bucket to hide her face. "They were right, you know. Chieftain goes his own way. He's Jane's pet and will only move when she coaxes him. And, as you noticed, I have no place with the Barn Rats." She began painting the tiny strips of wood between the panes. "I can walk, trot, and canter and can go over small fences as well as the Lavoies. But the clothes I wear don't have brand names, and my boots aren't leather."

"What you need is a plan to get your own horse," Sam advised. "I don't think trying to control an old, spoiled horse is teaching you *anything*."

Meg sighed. "You're right. But Mom says the house eats all the money. I have a dream where the front door opens and sucks Mom's and Dad's paychecks right out of their hands."

The girls laughed and worked in silence for a while. Then Sam said, "So give up the lessons and ask your mother to save that money for your horse fund."

Meg's brush wobbled, smearing the old, wavy

glass that probably had been there a hundred years. "Even if she saved all the money from my Saturday lessons, I figure I'd get my horse on my fiftieth birthday."

Sam jumped down. "When you're fifty you'll need an animal like Chieftain, slow and steady. Let's clean our brushes and air the room or I won't be able to sleep in here tonight."

They washed their hands in the kitchen sink before taking cookies from the plate Mrs. Madison offered them.

"Careful. They're still hot," Sam's mother said. "What do you think of that paint color, Meg?"

Meg swallowed a piece of the cookie as she tried not to laugh. "It's . . . it's . . . nice," she said finally.

The next morning, Meg found her mother out in the vegetable garden and hunkered down next to her. Kara sat in a sandbox her father had built, pouring sand through chubby fingers.

"Sam had the greatest idea," Meg began. "If I give up lessons at High Ridge, that lesson money could go in my horse fund."

Mom pushed back a strand of hair, leaving a streak of dirt on her forehead. "What horse fund?"

"The money you're saving to buy me a horse. We have a field and a bathtub, so a horse comes next." A bean plant came up with a handful of crabgrass, and Meg hastily patted it back in the earth.

Her mother yanked up a clump of weeds with more force than was needed, and almost fell backward. "Brad says all the field needs is a tractor, and Dan says it needs chickens. We moved here for space enough for the six of us to move around in. Not for things."

"A horse's not a thing. Besides, the boys are too young for tractors and chickens, but I'm the perfect age for a horse."

"Meg," her mother said, "I did not go back to teaching to buy horses or tractors. I have to work so we can eat, and fill up the oil tank, and pay the taxes. Teaching is important, but if I could choose, I would stay home and take care of Kara the way I took care of you when you were little. I'd have time to read. The house would be clean. I'd even have time to bake chocolate chip cookies." She laughed and pushed hair off her face, leaving another streak of dirt. "You and I both know that's not quite true. The house would never be clean. At least teaching has the same vacations and almost the same hours you children have. And it keeps me so busy I never have time to worry about the state of the house."

"But I'm right for a horse now," Meg insisted. "Next year I might start liking boys, or walk around with one of those headsets on, listening to music. I'm getting old. The field and I are ready for a horse."

"Dear girl. You are as persistent as these weeds. I will pay you a dollar to clear out this bean section. Consider it the beginning of your horse fund."

At least yesterday's rain had softened the ground, Meg thought. She could see the picture now. Today the beans, tomorrow the tomatoes. Maybe she would only be forty when she got her horse.

For the next week the schedule was working in the garden in the morning and painting Sam's room in the afternoon. "I think," Meg said as she put the final coat on the window frames, "that even migrant workers get more than a dollar for four hours of work."

"Count your blessings, Chicken Little. Every dollar adds to your fund. Consider how much we're not making, painting this room."

Meg cleaned the paintbrush carefully. The colonial blue woodwork looked just right for this little room with its slanting ceiling. "That's done. When's your mother going to do the papering?"

"Tomorrow. That means I'll have Tina all day."

Meg smiled. "Bring her over to play in the sandbox with Kara. Then you can help me in the garden. It's your fault I'm working, so you might as well work, too."

The next day Meg's mother offered lunch to Sam and Tina. "I know your mother is up to her ears in wallpaper paste. How about grilled cheese sandwiches?"

"Not a bad lunch for migrant workers," Meg muttered to Sam as they inched their way through the carrots.

Sam grinned. "I didn't know this was a garden before. The weeds were taller than the plants. Now it's beginning to look good. I think it needed a couple of migrant workers."

"At least workers who don't try to read when they're working, like Mom does. We've made our mark on two places this summer. This garden and your room. I can't wait to see it with the wallpaper up."

"This afternoon let's make a mark on your riding ring. With the little ones helping stamp, we ought to be able to keep the tall grasses down."

Kara was carried up for her nap, so only Sam, Meg, and Tina slid through the bars of the gate and walked to the rise in the field where they made a halfhearted attempt to trample the grass. "It's too hot," Sam said.

Meg agreed. "Let's take Tina and wet our legs in Kara's plastic pool."

They walked slowly back, stopping at the largest of the buildings in the field. Built of gray, unpainted wood, it had four window openings across the front and a shelf the length of the back wall. There was a door opening, but no door. "We call this one the turkey coop because turkeys are bigger than chickens." The structure had a roof, though they could see the sky through it in many places. "I figure my horse could use this for shelter if it wanted. The walls would cut some of the wind, even if there's no glass in the windows," Meg said.

"Wouldn't you keep your horse in the barn?" Good, Meg thought. Sam was beginning to believe in her dream.

"The floor is too bad. With all these buildings, there's not one fit for a horse." Meg tried to picture a horse sheltered in the ramshackle turkey coop, knew it wouldn't work, but kept that information to herself.

The building they called the chicken coop, because it was smaller, had a carpet of purple pigwort blossoms growing where the run used to be. It was the same weathered gray and had the same shelf along the back wall. Some of the windows still had chicken wire stapled to them. "I figure that shelf is where the chickens roosted and laid their eggs," Meg said.

The last little building was not big enough for a horse. "This is my house," Tina announced.

She walked in and sat on a broken kitchen chair.

"Maybe the McLaughlin children used it for a playhouse," Meg said. "When Kara gets bigger we could fix it up for the girls. We could hang curtains and find a rug to put down."

As they walked back to the gate, sharp sounds of hammers pounding came from the turkey coop. Brad sat on the roof, tearing the loose roofing off, while Dan swung at the side wall.

Meg raced to the coop. "What do you think you're doing?"

"Dad said we could. It's ours. We can do anything we want to it." Brad tore off more of the roof and flung it down.

"They're going to tear everything down." Meg watched helplessly as the roof of her horse's shelter opened wider to the sky.

"I want a house to tear down, too. I want to tear down my house," Tina cried.

Sam took a firm hold on Tina and headed for the gate. "We're going wading, little sister. Meg's in no mood to give you a house to tear down. Didn't you hear her say someday we'd make it into a playhouse?" She gave Meg an understanding look.

How lucky Sam was not to have brothers, though Tina could tear things down, too. Brad and Dan were going to fill the field with loose nails and sharp bits of wood, and tear down the turkey coop before she ever got a horse.

# 5

Meg's birthday on July fourth might not have the importance of Independence Day, but secretly she felt that the fireworks and parade were for her. The whole week before, she and Sam spent together, which made her so happy that when her mother asked who she wanted for her party, she said, "Just Sam. Save the money for my horse fund."

"How about those lovely girls at High Ridge?" her mother asked.

"If you'd only stay around during the lessons, you'd know they're not as lovely as they look. So many of my wishes are coming true. Last year my wish was for a house with a fireplace, so Santa could come down the chimney once before I got too old. This year I wished for a friend, and now I have Sam. There's just one big wish left."

Her mother patted Meg's hand. "Two out of three's a good start. I'm going to set everything up like a real party because I'm not ready to give up celebrating your birthday. July is such a lovely birthday month."

On the day of her birthday, Meg and Sam rode uptown in the van, loaded with Madisons and Kirtlands. Bill Kirtland, Meg's father, drove, with Brad buckled in the passenger seat. Sam's mother, Betty Madison, and Meg's mother, Janet Kirtland, rode with the rest of the children in the back, somehow managing to talk above all the noise around them.

The annual Independence Day parade was called the Horribles Parade. It wasn't horrible, though at some time in the past it might have been. It was just homemade, using every kind of vehicle available, decorated mostly with cardboard signs and crepe paper streamers. The parade always started at noon, so the two families unfolded chairs near the reviewers' stand to watch it from beginning to end. The town might be small, but the parade was not. The police chief rode in the lead patrol car, followed by fire trucks, all the town employees, the veterans, scouts, and the other groups. The Barn Rats rode horses that threatened to become unruly when caps exploded nearby. Local trucks crept up Main Street, crepe paper fluttering, with signs proclaiming local problems, such as sewer drains that didn't drain or a playgound without supervision. Children appeared everywhere, on the floats, running through front yards, and dripping ice cream cones on the sidewalks.

Tina sat next to Sam, and Meg tried to hold a wriggling Kara in her lap. "Where are the boys?" Meg's mother asked, realizing suddenly that their chairs were empty. Then she waved frantically as the Little League float went by, with Brad and Dan throwing candy kisses out into the crowd.

"They don't even belong," Meg said, feeling envious. How did they have the nerve to jump on a float and throw out candy?

"Next year," her mother said, "Brad can try out, and Dan the year after. That will mean more taxiing for me. Rides to practices and games."

"But you'll be saving so much money and time not taking me to High Ridge." Meg smiled at Sam.

"You've got such a perfect day for a birthday," Sam said. "Look, everyone's dressed in your favorite colors."

"Wait till they send up those fireworks tonight, that's even better." Meg felt pleased with her choice of birthdays, certain she had been born to the strains of "The Star-Spangled Banner."

"There's Pop," Tina yelled.

A pickup truck went by with a sign that read, "Plant trees in your park." The back of the truck was filled with small trees of different kinds, all strung with red, white, and blue bulbs that gleamed weakly in the summer sun. A man's arm waved from the driver's side.

"I still don't know what your dad looks like," Meg said. "And you never told me he works with trees."

"You never asked," Sam said. "He's trying to get a landscaping company going, but right now he takes care of the grounds at the junior college."

Meg watched the arm disappear into the cab and felt a twinge. The friendship she had with Sam was one-sided. Meg had done nothing but show off Meadowbrook Farm and talk about her horse. Birthday or not, it was time she paid more attention to Sam. She had to ask the right questions and listen to Sam's answers, and she had better start right away, before she lost her first good friend. "Tell me about your father," she said.

"Later," Sam said, her eyes on the next float.

That afternoon, Meg and Sam sat on the red windowsills overlooking the porch roof. Meg's father had driven both families home, then took off again, this time in his small car. Meg's mother piled the younger children in the van. "We just have a few things to pick up at the drugstore," she said with a wink at Meg.

"Okay. I want strawberry, vanilla, and blueberry," Meg said.

"I'll try, but don't count on the blueberry. You

know how few flavors the drugstore carries."

Kara sat in her car seat and clapped her hands. "Berry," she demanded.

The girls watched the van as it went down the road and disappeared.

"Well, you'll be blueberry enough," Meg said, looking at Sam's blue coveralls.

"And I think you've captured the strawberry market."

Meg wore shorts and shirt covered with a bright strawberry print. "Did you ever want something as badly as I want a horse?" she asked.

Sam nodded. "Not a thing you can buy. I want to run."

"Run?" Meg was puzzled. In all the days she'd known Sam, running had never been mentioned. "Like for president?"

"No. Run on a track team. At my last school, the high school was next door and I used to watch the team practice. I wanted so much to join them."

Meg stretched her legs. "Your legs are longer than mine. You'd be good at running. When I get my horse, we'll pace you."

"What if you don't get a horse?"

Meg shrugged. "I've lived this long without one. I guess I'll just go on dreaming. But I can borrow Dad's stopwatch and time you." She slid off the sill. "Come on, let's walk down the street and watch for the van. They have to bring the ice cream home fast in this heat."

She matched her steps to Sam's longer stride. Remembering her resolution of the morning to ask more questions and to listen harder, Meg asked, "How come you didn't tell me what your father does?"

"I don't know. He's just starting out here. There wasn't much landscaping business in Nova Scotia. So far there's not been enough business here to brag about, besides the junior college, but Pop's sure things will get better."

"Isn't it funny that our parents all work in schools?" Meg asked.

"I don't think teaching and gardening are much alike, even if Pop gardens at a school. Besides, my mother doesn't work at all."

Meg wanted to ask what Sam's mother did all day with only Tina to take care of, but decided she'd asked enough questions for one day. Besides, she had more important questions, like what her parents were going to give her on her eleventh birthday, and did they find blueberry ice cream in the drugstore?

"Here they come." Meg felt a flutter. They probably had her present in the van, and soon she'd see it. She and Sam ran up the street after the van, Sam beating her easily. When they got to the driveway, Brad and Dan jumped out of the sliding door, while Meg's mother unbuckled Kara.

"Pick up the packages, will you girls?"

Meg searched the van. Nothing there except the paper tablecloth and plates and some decorations in one bag, and ice cream in another. No big exciting package, nothing hidden under the seats. She scooped up one paper bag and left the other for Sam. "Where's Dad?" she asked her mother when she slid the van door closed.

"He'll be home in time for the party. I'll leave you to decorate the table while I take this ice cream in." She carried Kara and the ice cream into the house.

Meg and Sam wrestled with the aluminum folding table that had been stored in the shed, and set it on the grassy island in the middle of the circular driveway. The paper things were all red, white, and blue. Sam anchored the corners of the red tablecloth with stones. There were blue plates and white plastic forks and spoons. The girls sat on the grass and blew up balloons, tying them with string to the branches of the maple trees. "All we need is a cardinal and a blue jay on the snow to make this a perfect red, white, and blue day," Sam said with delight.

"There were no presents in the van. I'm afraid they'll put money in my horse fund. I mean, I want money in the fund, but it's my birthday. I want a birthday present."

"Well, if that's all you want, try this." Sam reached into her shirt pocket and drew out a small jewelry box. "Happy birthday, Meg."

Inside the box, nestled in velvet, was a silver horse. "Oh," Meg said, drawing in a breath. "I have a chain. I'll wear it always."

Meg put the charm back in the box and set it on the table. She looked at Sam, dear, thorough-bred Sam, and smiled until her cheeks hurt.

There was the sound of a motor on the road, moving up from Sam's house. Meg listened, glad her father was arriving in time for the party.

The boys spilled out of the house, followed by her mother and Kara. "Your father's coming. Put Kara in her stroller while I get the camera."

"To take Dad's picture?"

"He might have gotten a haircut," her mother said.

Curious, Meg thought. All her life her father had his hair cut and no one ever took his picture. And what barber opened up on the Fourth of July? She tumbled Kara into the stroller and wheeled her next to the table. Brad and Dan stood quietly, which Meg thought the strangest thing of all. A slight breeze fluttered the paper tablecloth, but otherwise they all stood without moving, waiting, waiting, for their father to come up the road.

A truck drove up to the driveway with the small car following close behind. A truck? Meg gasped and looked into Sam's eyes, but found no answers there. Sam shrugged her shoulders, as if to say, *Control yourself. It may not be what you think.* Meg looked again at the truck, watching carefully, warily, as it turned into the driveway, pulling a brown horse van behind it. Painted on the van in white script were the words, *Sky Farm.*

"Sam, do you see what I see?"

Sam put her hand to her mouth and nodded.

Her father pulled in next to the barn, while the driver stepped out of the truck. The two men walked around to the back of the horse van and lowered a ramp. A small, brown Shetland pony backed down the ramp, its coat gleaming in the July sunshine.

"You the birthday girl?" the man asked Meg. She nodded, unable to speak. "This here's your pony, then. Her registered name is Sky Farm's Arbutus. That's just a formality, though. I guess you can call her anything you want. I'm Jake Arsenius, the owner of Sky Farm. I gave your father and mother directions on how to take care of her, but I'm sure you'll have more questions. Call me anytime." He handed Meg the lead rope and a large manila envelope. "Those are her papers with instructions on how to file them, now that you're

48

the new owner. Better move her away so I can back up."

The world stopped spinning. The little breeze hushed. The sun hung heavy in the sky as Meg curled her fingers around the rope. She handed the papers to Sam.

Jake Arsenius from Sky Farm slammed his door, backed the truck, and headed down the road, across the stream, out of sight; leaving Meg holding the rope attached to the halter around the intelligent face of Sky Farm's Arbutus.

"Say something," Sam urged. "Are you all right?"

Meg shook her head. Her hand trembled so the rope nearly dropped to the ground. Suddenly she was smothered by arms as her parents hugged her.

"We couldn't wait until your horse account was big enough," her mother said. "We hope you like her. She's not quite a horse, but she is plenty big enough to carry you."

Meg stepped back. "But how could you? I mean, I know we don't have any extra money, and there are so many things this old farm needs more than it needs a pony."

Meg saw her mother's lips tremble into a smile. "I'm the culprit. Back when I was about your age, I wanted a horse, too. My parents gave me a bike, and I'll never forget how disappointed I was." She rubbed her eyes. "I got caught up in your dream, I guess, because it used to be my dream. Then the school paid me my summer salary in one lump check, and that helped me decide where the money should go."

Meg's father put his arm around his wife. "We were practical, though. Ponies cost less than horses, don't need shoes, and are healthier when they stay outdoors. Just like the ponies on the Shetland Islands or those ones you read about on Chincoteague. We've been having a good time driving around to different stables and finding things out."

Meg didn't care if it was a horse or a pony, a burro or a mule. It had four legs, a mane, and a tail, and now her field had a pony. She examined every sleek inch of the pony from soft nose to combed tail to neat hooves, marveling that the animal stood so quietly with so many people jostling around her.

"Come on, everyone. Let's show Meg's pony her new home," her father said as he helped Meg lead the pony to the field.

# 6

If Meg had eaten anything at her birthday party, she didn't remember. What kind of cake had it been, chocolate or white? All she remembered was her father helping her move the bars of the gate, unhitching the lead rope, and letting the pony loose in the field. Sam must have gone home, but Meg could not remember her going. Kara must have gone to bed. Someone cleaned up the red, white, and blue paper things while Meg sat on the gate and watched the pony explore her new home. Her father filled the big tub for the first time since the McLaughlins' cows had lived in the field and, when the sun dropped behind the pine trees, he led Meg into the house.

The manila envelope sat on the table next to the jewelry box. Sam must have carried them in. Meg had forgotten about the folder and now opened it to see what kind of papers came with a pony. There was an official-looking paper that

51

looked much like a diploma on the doctor's wall, but it had several branches on which were listed the sire and dam of Sky Farm's Arbutus. Above their names were their parents. Meg's father leaned over to look.

"It's a whole family tree," he said. "That's her breeding, and it's useful to know in case we're ever going to breed her. I'll put that in with the family papers so it won't get lost."

The other paper was a list of instructions for filling out a change of ownership, to be sent to the Pony Club of America. Mr. Arsenius of Sky Farm had signed his name, and Meg took her father's pen and signed her name as the present owner. There was also a book that gave the rules of the pony club.

Her father thumbed through the pages. "Ah, now I understand about the name. Her official name is Sky Farm's Arbutus, which was accepted by the pony club. Apparently they don't want two ponies to have the same name. It's like the kennel club for dogs."

"I understand the 'Sky Farm,' because that's where she came from, but what's an *arbutus*?" Meg asked.

"I'll show you one day," her mother said. "It's a flower that grows in the woods. It lies close to the ground and has little white or pink flowers and then red berries."

"There's another one I know," her father added. "It's called trailing arbutus. I've seen it growing under the pines."

Meg handed the papers to her father and then yawned. "Now I understand about the name. I'll call her Beauty, though. Like Black Beauty, only she's brown."

It was official. Meg was eleven, and Meg had a horse. Well, a pony. Nothing seemed real and the voices of her family came from a long distance away. She climbed the stairs to her room, certain she would not be able to sleep. But the minute Meg got into bed, she fell into a dream-filled world of miniature horses, demure and placid, who let her pet them and followed her around like ducklings. If there were fireworks to celebrate her birthday, she didn't hear them.

Meg woke to see the first rays of the sun, leaped into her clothes, and grabbed a muffin before heading out to the field. It was the first day she hadn't looked out the east window to where Sam's house was, but she was sure Sam would understand. The first day of her new life, with her own pony in the field.

The field seemed empty. Perhaps yesterday had been a dream. Meg's heart beat faster as her eyes searched out every hiding place. Calling "Beauty," she stepped in and out of the coops and around the crab apple trees. The discovery of small hoofprints by the stream quieted the thumping a little. She always imagined her horse hiding in the clump of trees, so she leaped the stream and fought her way through tangled branches that caught at her hair. Beauty had left a long strand of mane in that same spot.

Meg emerged from the trees and stopped. Straight ahead of her sat a young rabbit, and between the rabbit and the stone wall stood Beauty. Meg looked at the pony until her legs stopped shaking. She'd read that animals could sense a person's emotions, and she wanted Beauty to think of her as a calm person who knew what she was doing. Chieftain probably thought of her as wishy-washy, and that was why he wouldn't behave properly for her, or maybe she should have been bigger and heavier, and with a louder voice.

As if leading Meg away from the rabbit, Beauty walked along beside the wall, rounded the corner, leaped the stream, and continued along the edge of the field. Meg followed, certain that Beauty would soon stop and wait for her. Whenever Beauty cropped grass, Meg felt she gained a few steps, but then the pony moved again and Meg lost her advantage. At least the pony seemed to like the field and was not racing around looking for a way out.

"Patience, that's all it takes," Meg said to herself between her soft calls to Beauty. There were worse things to do on a summer morning than walk behind her own pony in her own field. But Meg was short on patience. The sun rose higher, and part of the first day of her new life disappeared with the morning.

Frustrated as she was, Meg took time to examine her pony from afar. Beauty looked like a miniature Arabian or thoroughbred, with a fine muzzle, small, well-pointed ears, delicate legs, and a glossy coat. Her mane and tail were soft and silky, the long tail almost trailing on the ground. The small hooves were perfectly formed, leaving round impressions in the soft ground near the stream. Meg had seen many ponies, but Beauty was an aristocrat.

On Beauty's second trip around the field, Meg decided it must be time for lunch. Stalking a pony did give one an appetite. The minute Meg turned away, she saw out of the corner of her eye that Beauty stopped to eat grass. She felt stirrings of anger, mixed with sadness. In her dreams, her horse had welcomed her, stood still for her to mount, and behaved like the horses in books. But Beauty probably was laughing into the summer grass. Meg slowly climbed the gate and headed for the house.

In the kitchen, her mother was feeding Kara. "Good. I was going to send Brad out to get you, Meg. It's time for breakfast."

"Breakfast? I came in for lunch."

"Maybe it is lunchtime for you. The sun comes up early in midsummer."

Brad and Dan sat outside on the back steps, eating cereal. Coffee perked. It felt good to be back in the normal world where things happened as Meg expected them to happen. She fixed a bowl of cereal and sat at the picnic table, deciding not to mention that Beauty would not let her come near. There were things they needed more than a pony, and she didn't want anyone to think she wasn't grateful.

"How are things in the old corral?" her mother asked, concern in her voice. "You don't usually sit down for breakfast. Is everything all right?"

"Fine. Fine." As fine as a ride on Chieftain, or as Sam's colonial blue paint.

"As soon as your father and I have had breakfast, I'll bring Kara out to watch you ride."

Cereal stuck in her throat, so Meg splashed in more milk. "Haven't ridden her yet. Thought I'd let her get used to me first."

"That's probably a good idea," her mother said. "I don't know anything about horses, but you have to start out slowly with any animal. We'll come out and watch you get acquainted."

56

The cereal gave Meg strength. She had to be more assertive, that was all. By the time her father finished breakfast, she'd be riding that little animal. On the way out the back hall she took her hard hat off its hook. She was not going to take any chances in a field full of granite chunks.

The sun was full-strength, as strong as she was. Meg put on her hat and climbed through the gate. Beauty ate grass, giving no sign she knew Meg was there. Meg had a full view of round rump and tail.

"Beauty," Meg said in a loud voice. "Beauty, come here." She stamped her foot strongly, but the sound of a sneaker hitting grass didn't frighten even a barn swallow who buzzed around Meg's head. Beauty continued to eat grass.

"Beauty, I order you to come here." Now *that* got her attention. Meg was certain she saw an ear twitch.

Speed might be the answer. Meg ran to where Beauty was standing, only to see her a minute later eating grass a few feet farther away. Meg ran after her again, determined this time to grab onto her mane, but the pony picked up her steps, first trotting, then cantering. Meg was smart enough to know that she could not outrun a pony, especially when she was already out of breath. She sat down on a warm rock and removed her hat.

Beauty perked up her ears at the sound of the family gathering at the gate. "At least a tractor lets you get on it," Brad yelled.

Meg walked to the gate. "She just walks away if I get near her. Not far, just far enough."

"Can you catch her, Bill?" her mother asked, looking as disappointed as if her own dream pony had turned obstinate.

"I don't think I'll try. Mr. Arsenius of Sky Farm didn't mention this would be a problem, Janet," he said. "I'm going over there this afternoon to check on what else she needs, and I'll see about how to catch her. Wish I knew as much about horses as I do about football. Want to come?"

Meg did not want to admit to the people at Sky Farm that she couldn't catch her own birthday present. "No. Sam will be over soon."

"Until Sam comes, I need some help in the garden," her mother said. "Any money you make will still go into the pony fund for Beauty's expenses."

Meg exchanged her hard hat for a straw one. Before going to the garden she made a quick trip to the shed behind the barn. It might make a stall for Beauty. Casually she kicked the rusty tools leaning against the wall. One of them caught her eye. It looked like an old-fashioned plow with a small wheel in front and two tall handles, but instead of a plow it had curved claws.

"What do you suppose this is?" she asked her mother, dragging it out of the shed.

"Why, Meg, it looks to me like an old-time cultivator you've got there. Wheel it between the rows and it should loosen the weeds and the earth."

It didn't work that easily, but Meg found it a great improvement over crawling around on her knees. The trouble was that she was not quite tall enough, and her hands were at an awkward angle.

"That is absolutely great," Sam said. "Let me try." Sam had run across the side yard and appeared at the edge of the garden. "I heard you talking out here and took a shortcut." She picked up the cultivator and soon had a row done. A few inches in height made the difference, and Meg followed Sam's path, picking up clumps of weeds. Two piles grew at the edge of the garden, one of stones, the other a mound of weeds.

"How's the pony? You haven't said one word about what was supposed to be the greatest thing in your life," Sam said.

"I heard that mules are stubborn. Well, ponies are stubborner."

"Oh. What's she stubborn about?"

"Being caught, for one thing." Meg answered. "I can't get close enough to find out what else she's stubborn about. I spent a year of Saturdays sitting on Chieftain, who didn't behave, and I just spent a whole morning walking behind a pony. Think you can help me?"

Sam walked the cultivator to the house and leaned it against the wall. "I've had my fill of helping. That is a great tool, though. The Mc-Laughlins knew how to do things right. We're going swimming at the state park. Want to come?"

The trip to the state park took all the preparation of a safari. Janet Kirtland dug out bathing suits, passed suntan lotion around, stuck towels in the back of the stroller, and since she had offered to drive, the family, minus their father, piled into the van. They picked up Betty Madison and Tina, and drove to the lake.

Meg and Sam walked sedately from the parking lot to the lake, watching Brad and Dan run to the water and dive in.

"They're cute," Sam said.

"You should try living with them." Meg thought they were like dolphins, rolling around joyously in the water, but what girl would admit she had cute brothers?

Meg and Sam swam out to the raft and practiced diving. "I'm glad your mother likes coming to the beach," Meg said. "Coming here with you gets Mom out of the house and away from her books."

"Let's go baby-sit so they can go in." Sam made a final dive, and soon she and Meg were sitting on towels, watching the little ones dig in the sand.

"Having a pony is not what I thought it would be," Meg confided secretly. "I need some kind of magic to capture Beauty. Strength or something. I wonder how I can get it. Maybe a person has to be born with it."

"Just don't try it on me," Sam said. "Sugar works better. Besides, babies get what they want, and they're not strong. Put a lump of sugar on your hand and hold it out."

"I could try sugar," Meg said thoughtfully. "That is, if I can get near enough for her to taste it."

"Give Beauty time. After all, you've only been at this half a day. I guess things are not always what you expect."

"You are so-o-o right." Meg flung her arms in great circles to get the knots out of her shoulders. "When we moved here I thought I'd be lonesome until I got to high school. And then look who moves in right next door."

"We came from a hick town in Nova Scotia to another hick town, and who is the first person I meet?" Sam asked. "A short horsey kid who now has a short horse in her backyard."

"Pony. Pony."

61

Meg and Sam stood up and linked arms. "Why don't you work with Beauty in the mornings and swim with us in the afternoons?" Sam suggested. "Sooner or later that horse is going to give in."

"Pony. Not horse," Meg said, feeling much better. Tomorrow she'd show Sam that she'd won Beauty over.

# 7

Meg didn't awaken until the sun hit her red wall. Beauty might not want to start the day too early, she told herself, not willing to admit that sleeping late would shorten the long morning of walking around the field after the wary beast. Meg glanced out the window at the pear trees and wished Sam would appear to help her get Beauty's attention. "No," she said, as she pulled on cutoff jeans and a knit shirt. "Beauty is mine, and I'm the one who has to catch her."

Even though the sun was high in the sky, Meg's sneakers turned dark with dew. She carried a pail with a layer of oats on the bottom, which the people at Sky Farm had recommended for catching stubborn ponies. Her father had warned her not to let Beauty have more than a handful, as ponies didn't need to be any more high-spirited than they already were. Mr. Arsenius said that ponies didn't need much more than grass or hay.

Sugar, molasses, or oats all made ponies too frisky. So much for Sam's idea of sugar, Meg thought. She would just use the oats to entice Beauty, and would let her have a taste as a reward for being caught. She thought Beauty had too much spirit as it was.

"Beauty. Come on, Beauty." Meg rattled the oats.

Beauty poised on delicate legs, pricked up her ears, then wheeled and galloped to the far end of the field.

"Here, Beauty, Beauty, Beauty," Meg coaxed. The pail hit her legs as she stumbled over clumps of grass.

The pony grazed quietly. Meg inched through the wet grass, cupping the handful of grain and letting it ping back into the pail. Four feet from the pony she could see the tiny white blaze just below the luminous dark eyes.

Beauty seemed to have an uncanny sense that allowed Meg to come within four feet of her. Then, if Meg advanced three steps, Beauty moved three steps away, all the while eating grass and seeming to pay no attention.

Meg became a cat, stretching out on lichened rocks, following Beauty with her eyes. She slithered off into the grass and left the pail as she crawled, first an arm out, then a leg. Beauty was not fooled, but whinnied and galloped past Meg's outstretched hand. The pony spun to a halt and dipped her nose into the pail. A fat tongue circled the bottom, collecting the grains.

"You . . . you blassifrax!" Meg raged. "Son of a sea cook! Dumbbell, trouble, meany!" Meg was running out of swear words. "You sprat!"

She picked up the empty pail and strode toward the shed. "I don't care," she yelled. "I don't feel like playing your games anymore." Not true. She did care. What was worse, she knew Beauty knew she cared. Beauty galloped off, fueled by two handfuls of stolen oats.

Meg took the pail into the cranberry shed and put it down next to the bag of oats. Mr. Arsenius was right. Ponies did like oats, and oats did make them frisky. Maybe tomorrow Beauty would be calmer. Meg's eyes blurred as she read the McLaughlins' diary on the wall. Penciled in were frost dates. *July 13, 1854. August 19, 1863.* No wonder they had difficulty farming Meadowbrook Farm. She wondered what old Ben would have done if he met up with Beauty. She imagined him going into the field wearing his three-piece suit, ordering the pony to come at once. Mr. Arsenius had raised the pony and she probably responded to a man's voice. Well, Meg was not a man, and Beauty would have to like her just as she was.

It was too early to eat lunch, so Meg changed hats and went out to grub in the garden.

Later that day, Meg and Sam sat in the shallow water of the lake, making a corral with their legs so Tina and Kara couldn't run into deeper water. Meg dribbled water over her arms. "Two days and I still can't get near that animal," she said. It was hard to admit, after all her bragging about what she'd do when she got her horse.

"Did you try sugar?" Sam asked.

"No, but I did try oats. I crept up on her and she licked the oats out of the pail and galloped away."

"How about a lasso?"

Meg giggled. "I think Beauty's an English pony, not a western one. Besides, I don't know how to rope an animal."

"Maybe Miss Jane or one of the Barn Rats could help."

Meg considered this. Miss Jane went to a night college, studying to be a lawyer, and didn't have much time to work with a stubborn pony. Callie might be the best person. She was calm and handled her pony well. But Meg hated the thought of giving up so soon. "I think I'll wait a while. Beauty's my present, and I have to be the one to ride her first."

Sam stood up. "Let's take the babies back to my mother so we can swim. All this sitting around is making me fat."

Meg watched Sam scoop Tina out of the water. There was not an ounce of fat under Sam's tank suit. Meg examined her own legs after two days of walking after Beauty, and found no fat on them, either. She picked up Kara and carried her, squirming, to Mrs. Madison's blanket.

July was passing quickly, and Meg had the feeling she stood on ground that slanted down into fall. Every eleven-year-old ought to be granted a year without school to experience the seasons and have a chance to learn about the plants and creatures in the world around them, Meg thought. She considered taking a petition around, but knew the grown-ups would just laugh at a bunch of kids who couldn't vote yet.

Every day Meg walked confidently into the field regardless of the weather. Beauty was outside in sunshine or rain, eating grass or galloping around in a solitary way. She was not alone, though. Sometimes a small brown bird sat on her shoulder while she ate, and other times Meg caught sight of a female pheasant with her trailing brood or, now and then, the rabbit deep in the lush grass.

Bored with stalking Beauty, Meg put straw into the chicken coop in case the pony wanted to go inside. But though Beauty occasionally walked in, she walked right out again. Neither pouring rain nor hot sun persuaded her to stay in the coop.

Meg rolled apples into Beauty's path, or dropped carrot chunks on the riding ring. They always disappeared, but Meg never saw Beauty eating them.

One week it rained every day, swelling the stream so no water was needed in the tub. Meg's sneakers never dried. But still the pony eluded her.

Sam walked into the field on the first sunny day. She climbed over the gate and jogged up to the ring, where Meg doggedly stamped out new grass in the circle.

"Just another month and we'll be back in school," Sam said. "I can't wait. Pop's underfoot most of the time when it rains. Tina babbles to her dolls, for gosh sake. No swimming, no weeding your garden, and no running."

"The rain didn't slow me down," Meg said. "I've been out here every day, getting nowhere, as usual. Why don't you run in my ring? Beauty's over there." Meg tossed her head in the direction of the stream.

"Still stubborn as always?" Sam began a slow lope around the ring with Meg following her, in rhythm with the sound of hammering on the turkey coop. The boys were at it again.

"I yell at her, and it makes the same impression as rain on her back. Nothing."

The girls worked their way around the circle,

Sam increasing speed. The next time Meg looked, up, Beauty had moved closer as if curious about what these humans were up to. Meg kept her eyes on the track, ignoring the pony as the pony ignored her. Meg ran full out to keep up with Sam, but quick glances assured her that Beauty was definitely interested, though she put on a good show of eating grass.

"I can't stand it any longer," Meg said when Sam slowed down. "She's getting curious, and I think she wants to give in, but she doesn't seem to know how."

A crash like thunder, and a cry of "Watch out!" sent Meg and Sam running toward the coop while Beauty galloped around the crab apple trees.

Brad jumped up and down, exulting, "I did it. The center pole was holding up the whole thing."

The turkey coop lay on the ground, roof, walls, doors, and windows all flat, a pile of gray wood. Dust settled. Meg suddenly remembered that usually both her brothers were working. "Where's Dan?"

Dan lay close to the wreckage, his face as gray as the dust that covered him. He clutched his left arm and twisted his face. Tears furrowed through the dirt. At least he was breathing, and his head looked all right.

Meg squatted down. "Go get Dad or Mom! Get someone! I'll watch him," she told Brad, but Sam was already running toward the house.

Dan's eyes rolled up and he moaned a shocked, "Oh-h-h . . . " which scared Meg until she looked where Dan was looking. Beauty stood close to Dan's head and was calmly chewing on his hair.

In almost a month, Meg had never gotten closer than four feet to this animal who belonged only to her, and here Beauty was, close enough to Dan to eat his hair. "Oh, brother," Meg said, not quite sure to which one she spoke.

After the excitement of a trip to the doctor, including X rays and a cast from Dan's elbow to his hand, Meg sank onto the couch where Dan was lying and patted his leg. "I think, Mom," she said to her mother, who sprawled in a chair, sneakers up on the coffee table, "I think we should sell Beauty to pay the doctor bills."

"You can't sell that baby," Dan protested. "She likes me."

"That's why I think she should go. She has no loyalty. She doesn't even like me. This whole month she pretended I wasn't there. Then you lie down on the ground and she comes close enough to eat your hair."

"Oh, Meg." Her mother sounded tired. "I can't go back to hearing about how much you and the field need a pony. Give her time. Who knows? Tomorrow she might eat *your* hair."

*　　*　　*

Meg called Sam the next morning. "I've made up my mind. Beauty ate Dan's hair yesterday. It's time she was tamed."

"Is he all right?" Sam asked, sounding a little bewildered.

"He broke his arm and it's in a cast, but he's frisky as ever."

"I mean, how's his hair?"

Meg laughed. "She just nibbled on it. He still has it all. But if she got that close to Dan, I should be able to get that close to her."

"I'll help, if you're sure you want to catch her."

Meg was sure.

Meg was out in front, waiting for Sam to run up the road. Brad was tossing pebbles into the stream while Dan sat on the road with a fishing line dangling in the water. He didn't seem at all bothered by the cast on his arm.

"There're no fish down there," Meg said.

"That's all right," Dan said. "I don't like fish anyway."

Meg looked down at his pony-nibbled hair and tried to keep from laughing. "Want to play cowboys and help me catch the beast?"

Dan's brown eyes sparkled with excitement. "Count me in."

Brad was more cautious. "Does she kick?"

"You don't have to get that close. But I figure

71

if we get behind her and walk slowly toward the gate, she'll move away from us and get trapped by the shed. No cap guns or extra noise. Just sort of ease her into the corral, men."

Sam joined the posse and they all followed Meg. She went through the shed and picked up the tack her father had bought from Mr. Arsenius. A western saddle and a bridle and bit, which had never been used by Beauty. She carefully placed them on the gate before leading Sam, Brad, and Dan down toward the stream.

"We'll follow the far wall back to where Beauty is and make a semicircle. If you move quietly and keep a steady pace, she should keep her distance and walk toward the gate." Meg's heart pounded as she led the way. She worried that the boys might let out war whoops and scare Beauty, but they seemed impressed with the importance of what they were doing.

Sam waited and walked behind Dan just in case he broke into engine noises or hurt his arm again. Beauty ignored the line of stalkers, turning her back to them when they ranged behind her.

The four faced the gate and moved step by step across the field. Beauty calmly walked away from them. Inch by inch they walked forward, drawing closer together as they approached the gate. Beauty turned at the last minute when she couldn't go any farther, but Sam was there, reaching out a quiet hand. Meg grabbed her halter. Brad and Dan backed away, ready to run, but Beauty dropped her head and stood still. The game was over and she seemed to know it.

"Come pat her nose," Meg urged the boys. Hesitantly they reached up and patted her gently while Sam held the halter. Meg had often bridled Chieftain, but her hands shook as she removed the halter and worked the bit between Beauty's teeth. When the bridle was smoothly arranged, she lifted the saddle and set it on Beauty's back, tightening the straps under the belly. Beauty seemed to say, *All right, you caught me. Now what are you going to do?*

Meg had no question in her mind. She mounted the pony, adjusted the stirrups, and took the reins from Sam. "Thanks, you guys," she said to her posse. "Giddyup, Beauty," she yelled, and Beauty did. She tossed her head and swished her tail, and reached out those slim and marvelous legs, all without so much as a kick from Meg's rubber boots. The two summer companions thundered around the entire field, from stream to coops, past rocks and crab apple trees, until Beauty stopped back at the gate.

"You did it!" Sam said, her face one big smile.

"We did it!" Meg answered.

"Yay," yelled the boys.

Meg rose before dawn and sneaked out of the house before anyone stirred. The morning was hers, the field, and Beauty. Only Beauty was not in sight when she climbed through the fence. Nothing moved along the stone wall. No tail swished near the stream. Meg walked slowly through the dewy grass, then in a panic began to run. Past the battered turkey coop, across the stream, through the thicket; then she stopped.

Beauty lay on the grass, head down, eyes closed, legs stretched out. She was dead, Meg thought. No. The round belly moved up and down. Meg bent down and put her arms around the pony's head. Beauty opened her eyes and seemed to smile. Then she stretched, scrambled to her feet, and stood placidly like the ponies in Meg's dream.

Meg grabbed the halter and pulled herself up onto the smooth back. She gripped her knees and gave a Tarzan yell of triumph. They galloped back to the gate for the saddle and bridle.

Early morning became Meg's secret time when she and her pony were in the field, so early that few birds stirred and mist rose from the stream. All she could hear was the pony's soft breathing and the soft thud of her hooves in the grass. Sometimes Beauty would play the old game and move away from Meg, or kick up her heels and outrun her. More and more, though, she waited by the gate and nickered softly when Meg appeared.

Meg tried to describe how beautiful the mornings were to Sam, but caught a look in Sam's eyes. "What's the matter?"

"I don't know," Sam said. "It's just that we don't do it together."

"You could come up and ride her, too."

Sam shook her head. "No. The mornings are yours. Funny how a part of me feels that I live in your house and want to be in your family."

"I felt the same way when you moved in. I'd think of you having breakfast, and wish I were there, away from the boys. But they're not so bad these days. I think they liked the roundup."

"I like the boys," Sam said. "I had a brother. He was between me and Tina. He got very sick and then he died. We don't talk about him anymore, but I think about him every day."

"Oh." Meg didn't know what to say. She had never imagined life without Brad and Dan, except to think of peace and quiet and clean rooms, and the turkey coop with a roof.

She felt sorry that Sam had lost her brother, and sorrier that her mornings did not include Sam. Her most precious private times with Beauty had nothing to do with anyone else, and that made her sad. She took Sam's hand and squeezed it. "You're my best friend, forever and ever."

"And you're mine. I just wish I were a horse sometimes, so I could really be your best friend."

That sounded so silly they both burst into giggles.

# 8

On the first day of school, Meg woke to the sound of her alarm. It was dark in the room, but she had laid out new school clothes the night before. She dressed quickly and ran out of the house before anyone stirred. Beauty stood waiting by the gate.

"You should have come to me that first morning. Now we have less time to spend," Meg whispered into Beauty's ear. "You're going to be lonesome today with everybody gone." She kissed the pony's muzzle and went back into the house. Lights were on, water ran, Kara's footsteps padded overhead. The new school year had begun.

The family scattered, with Meg's father driving to his school while Meg's mother dropped Kara off at play group on the way to her school. Brad and Dan set off down Elm Street to catch the bus to Woodland School, which housed kindergarten through grade three. Sam and Meg would take a different bus to Nearing School for fourth-, fifth-, and sixth-graders. The six Kirtlands went to five different places.

Meg walked down Elm Street behind Brad and Dan, whose bus picked them up first. Brad, with his dark eyes and brown hair spiky from the haircut Mom gave him at the beginning of summer, walked with confidence, wearing a navy shirt and gray pants. Dan, his light brown hair waving softly, followed behind with more reluctance. He held his left arm stiffly, though the cast had come off weeks before. Meg seldom noticed how her brothers dressed but admitted they were acceptable on the first day of school.

Peering down, she admired her own new rust-colored jumper and checked blouse. After a summer of grubbing and stalking, it was a pleasure to wear new, crisp clothes.

Sam came out of the Madison house wearing a jumper and blouse similar to Meg's. "Clarendon's?" Meg asked.

Sam nodded. "We couldn't have picked out anything more alike if we'd gone shopping together. Knowing I'm dressed like you are makes the first day in a new school easier to take."

Meg smiled. A summer with a best friend and already they picked similar clothes. Sixth grade would be a snap if they were in the same class. "Beauty waited at the gate this morning. I think she knew we wouldn't have our morning ride."

"Maybe horses are smarter than I thought they were."

"Ponies, ponies," Meg protested.

Meg and Sam dawdled on the way home, their new jumpers not as crisp in the hot September sun. "What great luck to be in the same class, even though Vanessa's there, too."

"Don't let her get to you," Sam said.

"Well, when I told her I'd gotten a pony, she didn't need to call Beauty a runt when she hadn't even seen her."

"The class is great, even if she's in it. Sitting next to you I didn't feel that it was the first day in a new school." Sam shifted her armload of books.

"Want to come over? I'll be riding."

"Sure. Soon as I change into shorts and show my mother these books. She warned me school might be harder here, and I think she's right." Sam went into her house, and Meg continued up Elm Street, stopping briefly to watch the thick, muddy brook trickle under the road. She'd have to start filling the tub on the weekend unless it rained soon.

What a relief to have the first day of school over. Meg stretched out her arms and smiled at the blue September day. Her bus got her home first, so she carried the door key. She would have a few quiet minutes to change her clothes and get something to eat before the boys came home. By the time her mother and Kara arrived, she would be riding.

Meg's joy disappeared when she reached the driveway. Right in the grassy center, where she had had her birthday party in July, Beauty calmly nibbled grass. She was not in her field.

Meg hoped there wouldn't be a repeat of the summer, with Beauty moving off when Meg approached. Pretending to be calm, talking softly above her beating heart, she murmured, "Beauty, here Beauty."

Beauty nickered and looked straight at Meg. She walked forward in an unhurried way and stuck her muzzle in Meg's outstretched hand.

"Oh, Beauty," Meg said, a rush of tears surprising her. "You did miss me." Gently she took hold of the halter and led the pony back through the opened gate. In the shed she found a length of rope, looped it around gate and fence, and tied a square knot.

Now that Beauty was back where she belonged, Meg went in to change clothes and grab a couple of apples. She took her hard hat off the hook and left the door unlocked for Brad and Dan.

Sam stood on the driveway, and Beauty nibbled grass in the center.

"Do you always let her loose like that?"

"Of course not. I just tied the gate with the rope." The rope lay on the ground by the gate. "Beauty," Meg wailed, "how are we going to keep you in the field?"

Beauty seemed to recognize her name and ambled over to sniff Meg's apple. Meg held it out on her open palm and the pony nipped it up in her teeth. "Here, Sam, you take the other apple before she gets too greedy. I'll get her ready to ride. When Dad comes home he'll have to figure out what to do with the gate."

The pony still chomped as Meg led her back into the field and shut the gate. Beauty stood quietly while Meg removed the halter and put the bit in her mouth. Meg felt more secure, but wondered if Beauty would escape the field every day.

She put on the saddle blanket, then lifted the saddle. The pony was only too ready for the daily ride, seven hours later than usual. Meg mounted and found the stirrups.

"Now that school has started, I've got to start training her. We'll take one lap around the field and then work in the ring."

Sam pitched the apple core and began to lope beside them as Beauty trotted around the edge of the field.

Sam's long legs had no trouble keeping up with Beauty's trot, but when Meg let her out into a full gallop around the ring, Sam sank to the grass. "Great workout. If we do this every afternoon for a year, I'll be in fine shape."

Meg slowed the pony to a walk. "I need more experience to train her right. Wish I could take her to High Ridge a couple of Saturdays. The horse fund went for the saddle and bridle, and when the grass dies in the wintertime we'll have to buy hay. I'm broke."

The girls walked Beauty back to the gate, where they curried and brushed her and Meg checked her hooves.

"Why don't you ride her over some Saturday and take a lesson? I could lend you some of my allowance," Sam said.

"It would take all morning to walk her over there. She'd be pooped. Besides, she's not shod." Meg took the saddle into the shed. "Honestly," she said when she came out, "I'm afraid to ride her on a street with cars whizzing by." Meg knew it wasn't the whole truth. Even Nicole would have a chance to look down on her when she was on Beauty. The thought was so disloyal that Meg's cheeks heated up. She adored Beauty and was proud of her, but a Shetland was not a horse, and the two snobby sisters would think of ways to torment her.

The days became full with school all day, workouts with Beauty in the afternoon, and more homework at night than Meg had ever had before. Meg's father had nailed the gate shut, so Beauty waited each afternoon in the field. Sam spent most afternoons with Meg, doing stretching exercises while Meg saddled her pony, then running with them around the edges of the field. From the cranberry shed to the stone wall, strands of smooth wire stapled to fence posts marked the edge directly behind the farmhouse. Stone walls on the side nearest Sam's house were too high for the pony to jump, and more stone walls barricaded the back of the field. Then wire fencing made up the other side and the front until meeting up with the wooden gate. The field was a giant rectangle, with the gate in the center of the front and attached to the shed. Meg checked the wires and gate every day, grateful she didn't have to chase after Beauty on the street.

After a turn around the borders, Sam did her cooling down exercises while Meg and Beauty worked in the ring. Meg pretended she was Miss Jane, calling out "Walk," or "Trot," taking care that Beauty was always on the right lead.

October was a glorious month with only an occasional day of rain. The maples in the center of the driveway cast a yellow light into the kitchen, and the leaves of the rambling roses on the rocks became as scarlet as the five-leaved quinquefolia.

Beauty ignored the crab apples beneath the trees, probably having tasted one which had puckered her mouth and sent her running for a drink of water.

Brad and Dan gathered boards from the fallen coop to break into kindling for winter fires in the fireplace. Ever since the roundup Brad had shown more interest in the pony.

"Want to ride her?" Meg asked him one chilly afternoon.

"Way to go," Dan encouraged Brad, who climbed into the saddle with Meg's help. She led them once around the ring, then Brad insisted on going alone.

Meg handed him the reins, and he gave a kick. Beauty moved from a walk to a trot, then stopped suddenly. Brad dropped into a pile of manure.

He got up, his eyes squinting from the smell, his lips tight. "If it doesn't have a motor, I say the heck with it."

Sam and Meg carefully kept from laughing until he crawled through the fence. "I do believe she does things on purpose," Sam marveled. "How did she know just where that manure pile was?"

Dan wiped his hands in a way that showed he wasn't interested in riding. He picked up a pile of wood and followed Brad out of the field.

Meg shook her head. "Ponies are ten times

smarter than horses," she said with pride.

Her mother was not quite as pleased with Beauty's performance. "I'm the one who wanted a horse, but it seems I can't get out in the field to watch you ride. Now I've got another load of clothes to wash. The boys can go out to collect wood, but they're to stay away from manure piles. Do you understand?"

Laughter brimmed in Meg's eyes, but she nodded solemnly. "I don't think they're the horsey type, especially when it comes to manure. I'll read to Kara while you do the wash. Maybe some weekend you'll come out and ride Beauty."

"I'm afraid my legs might touch the ground, and I'm probably too heavy." Meg's mother sighed and picked up the laundry basket. "But we have a long weekend coming up on Veterans Day, and I may try her out then."

Meg woke in the dark on Veterans Day, remembered there was no school, and fell asleep again. She did not move until the sun reached in her window.

On school days she could dress in minutes, but waking late made her sluggish and indecisive. Was Sam going to wear jeans to the parade? Where was that hairbrush? When she got to the kitchen, the family was milling around, eating, and she was trapped into pouring cereal for Kara as well as a bowlful for herself. One could lose half a day with this nonsense.

She was about to leave her bowl in the sink, when her mother said, "Help me clear this up, Meg. Beauty can wait a few minutes."

More than a few minutes. Meg washed and the boys dried, in between hitting each other with flicks of towels. She dried her hands finally, and her mother appeared with a basket of wet clothes. By the time the clothes were hung, the sun was high in the sky.

Meg climbed through the gate, checking to see that the long nails her dad closed it with were undisturbed. Gouges of white showed where Beauty worried at the gate while everyone was in school. Everything was intact, but Beauty did not greet her as she usually did each school morning.

"Beauty, here Beauty," Meg called. A blue jay answered. A red squirrel chased its mate around a crab apple tree. The roar of a jet sliced the quiet of the field.

"Maybe she's mad at me. She expects me at dawn."

Meg walked the regular route down to the stream, following the path that Beauty had pounded out. Beauty might be down on the ground, a delicate leg twisted under her. She might have a chill like Black Beauty had, or a cold like the cold that killed the Red Pony. Meg was afraid to look in the long grass, afraid not to look. Black muck at the edge of the stream pulled at her sneakers. A perfect small hoofprint was outlined in the mud.

"Might be there from yesterday's ride," she cautioned herself, but hope rose, a warm bubble inside her. A cluster of hoofprints headed south along the stream, and where the stream flowed under the wire fencing, a clump of mane fluttered in the wind.

Beauty was out of the field again, but this time not through the gate. Meg crawled under the wire and followed the stream to the road. There were no more hoofprints. She ran down Elm Street past Sam's house, as far as the bus stop, calling whenever she had enough breath. No friendly nicker answered.

Meg plunged back toward the house, sobbing to the slap of her sneakers. How could she have lost the one thing she wanted more than anything else in the whole world? What if she never saw that stubborn, charming, smart little pony again? An aching, empty hole filled her as she thought of the field without any animal in it. Beauty had run away.

Meg's father called the police chief. "He's got all his men out blocking off the parade route. No time for stray ponies. Couldn't understand how we could even ask at a time like this. With the police tied up, it would be a great day for a crime wave. Well," he reached for his football jacket, "let's take the van and look. Put some oats in a pail, Meg."

"Will you check around here?" Meg asked Brad. "Just go out to the main road and hunt for her?"

"Pony, pony, pony. That's all I ever hear around here. I'm sick and tired of it. Now, tractors, they don't run away or dump people in manure."

"Thanks a *lot*," Meg said, heavy on the "lot." "When your tractor runs out of gas, don't come running to me."

Brad shined up an apple. "Me and Dan, we could be orphans. You get all you want and there's nothing left for us." He smiled a wicked smile. "But if I stumble over your Beauty, I'll sure tell you about it."

Meg put the pail in the back of the van, then climbed into the front seat, so angry that for a minute she forgot to worry about Beauty. Anyone who chose a tractor over an animal was crazy.

The van groaned in second gear. Her father watched on the left, and Meg on the right. Hadn't she given Beauty all the love in the world? Didn't she have a whole field to herself? Hadn't she given her water and brushed her till she gleamed? What more could an animal want?

"We checked the fences, Dad. How come they didn't hold her? They held McLaughlin's cows."

"I don't think cows have as much imagination as ponies," her father said. "They just didn't think of getting out. But Beauty, she thinks. When she wants to stay in, she stays, and when she wants to get out, she goes."

Meg thought of Beauty's escapes when everyone went back to school, and of her dumping Brad in the manure pile. Beauty certainly did think.

The van turned onto the main road, where policemen were putting up sawhorses with detour signs. Clusters of Cub Scouts, Brownies, and the high school band were gathering. At least no pony was messing up the parade. Not yet, anyway.

Meg swallowed a scream. Maybe they were going the wrong way. A smart pony like Beauty would not have gone through town on the day of the parade. She would have gone to Upland. Her dad drove up a side street, out of the parade route, toward Middleford. Why would a pony want to go to Middleford?

"It's all my fault. I didn't take care of her right, otherwise she would have liked the field." Meg kept her eyes on the side of the road, but was sure Beauty would have gone the other way. She saw exactly what she expected. Nothing.

"I don't know anything about horses, but I suspect that ponies are different. They're smarter.

They are curious. According to the man at Sky Farm, ponies don't need much, so I think you gave her everything she needed. She just had to see what was on the other side of the fence."

They were now five miles out of town. Houses were farther apart. Trees and bushes at the side of the road offered thousands of hiding places for an errant pony. She could catch her halter on a wire or a branch and starve to death before anyone found her. She could stumble into an abandoned well, or break a leg in a woodchuck hole. Meg wished she could stop thinking, could stop picturing Beauty lying on her side, eyes glazed, blood channeling from her mouth.

Now they were ten miles out of town. "How far can a pony travel?" Meg asked.

"Beats me. We'll go into Middleford and ask the police there to keep an eye out for her. Then we'll turn back and go home to see if anyone's called."

Meg itched to turn around. She knew they were headed in the wrong direction. Why hadn't they started their search the other way? All ponies would certainly choose to go to Upland instead of Middleford.

Around the corner they passed a small used-car lot. The farmhouse next to the lot was almost invisible in a clump of trees. But what was visible was a small shaggy pony tied to one of the trees, its nose deep in the fallen leaves.

"Beauty." Meg almost burst with relief. The van lurched to a stop. A gray-haired man opened the front door of his house in the trees and smiled as he walked toward them.

"Thought someone might be lookin' for this critter. She dropped in no more'n half an hour ago and acted like she owned the place. Sometimes the little devils kick, but this'un comes up nice as pie and talks to me. I grabbed the halter and took my belt, bein' the only thing handy, and tied her to the tree."

"Thank you, thank you." Meg tumbled out the door, not knowing whether she was going to hug the pony or yell at her for scaring her half to death.

"Beauty, why did you run away?"

The pony found an apple under the leaves and crunched it loudly.

"Don't you love me?"

Beauty's stomach rumbled. Meg figured she'd had too many apples that morning.

Meg's father fastened the lead rope to the halter and handed the belt back to the man, who hitched up his baggy pants with a sigh of relief.

"You've got quite a walk ahead of you, Meg," her father said. "Ten miles coming out here, but longer going back. You'll have to take her around town on Oak Street, not down the parade route. It never occurred to me that a little animal like this could travel so far. I'll pick up the saddle and bridle and meet you, either on this road or on Oak Street."

He put the van in gear and waved out the window. "Thanks very much for catching her," he said to the man. He drove out the driveway and turned the corner toward home.

Meg felt a stab of terror. What dangers hid along the road? Fierce dogs, speeding cars, or wild animals in the woods?

She and her living, breathing, rumbling pony walked on the left-hand side of the road, facing traffic. Meg kept Beauty on the inside to protect her from the cars and keep her feet off the pavement, but the inside was where the good grass grew. Beauty dropped her head to graze and Meg pulled on the lead rope until she felt her left arm had grown longer than the right. She tried riding, but found that a lead rope on a halter did not direct a stubborn pony as a bridle and bit did. Meg jerked the rope and tugged, coaxed and ordered, wept and fumed, for five long, dusty miles.

Meg recognized the sound of the van before she saw it. Her father had brought water for both of them, and while Meg sat at the side of the road, he saddled and bridled Beauty.

"I didn't know you could do that," Meg said.

"If you have kids, you learn all kinds of things." He gave Meg a leg up and patted her shoulder. "Take it easy and ride carefully."

The sun had dropped behind the pines before pony and rider reached the driveway. Her dad helped Meg open the gate, then nailed it shut behind the inquisitive pony. "Come help me with the wire I'm adding over the stream," he said.

Meg missed the lunch she never had, her fingers stung from the cold, and her throat was drier than the inside of a haystack. She helped hold the wire while her father stapled it to the posts.

"See that down there, under the pear trees?" Her father pointed to a small green plant with red berries. "There's your arbutus. It's a neat little plant."

"It's kind of like Beauty," Meg said. "Small, but colorful. Does what it wants." Except, she thought, it couldn't run out of the field.

"Think she'll do it again, Dad?"

"Every gate and every wire is a challenge to her. You can bet your sweet life she'll try it again." He pulled the wire taut. "We'd better spend our weekends checking out this fence," he said, his mouth set in a grim line.

"And I guess I'll have to keep my regular schedule every day, holiday or not."

Meg's dad clapped her on the back. "That's my girl. Today was not what you'd call a restful holiday. I've got a football game tomorrow, you know." His broad shoulders seemed a little hunched as he carried the tools back to the shed.

Meg thought sadly of the riding lesson she'd promised her mother. They'd do it tomorrow, she decided, because she was too tired and Beauty must be, too.

Beauty nickered, nudging Meg with her nose.

"You can't possibly want me to ride you now. Not after all I've been through today. Hours of thinking you were dead, hours of searching, and to top it off, a ten-mile walk."

The shaggy head pushed at Meg's sleeve. Meg moved slowly back to the shed and got the saddle and the bridle, still warm from their trek home, and went to work.

"You clown," Meg said through gritted teeth. Beauty let out a sigh of air and seemed to smile. "Just tell me one thing," Meg said. "Which of us is the master and which is the pet?"

Beauty whinnied shrilly. Meg pulled herself into the saddle and trotted her master to the exercise ring.

# 9

Winter sneaked in before Thanksgiving. Grass crackled and shattered under foot, and Beauty snorted clouds of steam. Ice thickened in the tub and had to be chunked out with stabs from the iron pipe. When Meg left the field in early darkness, Beauty followed her, nickering softly. Meg kissed the furry face and rubbed the blaze.

"Why Beauty, you're lonesome."

Beauty's head dropped before the wind. The field looked desolate, leafless, and dead. The Sky Farm man had said ponies did not need shelter, but Meg sadly surveyed the torn-down turkey coop and wished the boys had not found the main beam.

"Beauty's lonely," Meg announced when she sat down for dinner. "I wish Sam had a horse we could keep in the field with her." She caught her parents glancing at each other, like two kids passing notes in school. Her mother nodded slightly.

"What? What?" Meg demanded.

"We didn't want to say anything," her father said, "in case it didn't happen."

"In case what didn't happen?"

"When we picked Beauty she had already been bred."

"Bred?" Meg asked stupidly.

"How can a horse be bread?" Dan asked.

Mr. Kirtland ignored him. "If it took, and all goes well, come spring Beauty should have a foal."

Her mother leaned across the table. "For now this is our secret, Meg. Neither your father nor I know anything about a pony, or how to tell if she's going to have a baby. No use getting everyone excited about something that might not happen. Besides, spring's a long way off. By then we should know more."

"But I know you went to the doctor when you were going to have Kara. Shouldn't we do something?"

"Mr. Arsenius says there's nothing to worry about. Shetlands have babies in the field and don't need any help."

Meg tucked the secret warmly inside of her, sorry only that she couldn't tell Sam.

The next morning she carried a bucket of water that hit her shin as she walked, and dumped it into the tub before she examined Beauty carefully. The round belly seemed the same as it had the day she arrived. If Beauty was carrying a foal she, too, was keeping it a secret.

Winter turned brutal. Beauty stood in the chicken coop with her tail hanging out the open doorway, her nose clouding the air at the window, greeting Meg with a whinny when she got home from school. Meg guided the pony through the paths her hooves had carved in the snow. The hose froze completely, so every morning Meg filled buckets at the kitchen sink and carried them out to the tub. After school the water was frozen and she carried more buckets.

Beauty changed from a pony to a teddy bear. Her coat had started to grow in the fall, but now it hung long and shaggy with feathers of hair around her hooves.

"That's not a pony, she's turned into a donkey." Sam curried the shaggy coat while Meg checked the hooves for bits of ice. The girls were still warm from a run around the field, but it wouldn't take long in the dwindling light for their fingers to freeze up.

"A warm stable would be easier on us grooms," Meg said, stamping her feet to keep feeling in them.

"But what would she do? Stand all day in the stall?" Sam looked the pony over. "She's happy out there, and healthy, too."

97

"That makes two of us." Meg said. "Last year I had a bad throat from fall to spring, and Mom had to stay home with me and use up all her sick days. So far this year I've been out in every kind of weather, and my throat's just fine."

"I feel great, too. That pony's going to make a runner of me yet." Sam banged the curry comb against the gate. "Not much dust out here in the winter. She's clean."

They each carried a bucket of water out, then threw out some hay. Beauty turned her back on them and began to eat.

At Christmastime the weather warmed, raising clouds of mist from the rapidly melting snow piles. "This is crazy," Meg said, examining the ground. "Thanksgiving was colder than this, and it's too early for the January thaw." Rivulets of water ran beneath the snow, and patches of ice gleamed in the misty light. "I'm not even going to ride her until the ground is bare, or there's firm snow underfoot."

Sam slid down the path on rubber boots. "The only place I'm going to run is on the road. Vacation, and there's nothing to do."

Meg brightened. "We could work on the shed. Fix up that back room. Make proper pegs for the tack like they have at High Ridge."

"Curtains," Sam said.

"No curtains. Tack rooms never have curtains. You wouldn't want curtains, would you Beauty?"

Beauty swished her tail, a definite no.

The back room of the shed had been the Mc-Laughlins' workroom, with a workbench under the windows, stretching from one door to the other. On the other side was the old potbellied stove. Various tools and odds and ends of things cluttered the floor and were strewn on the bench. The disorder did not fit Meg's image of old Ben, but a whole generation had lived there after he died.

"Wouldn't it be fun to build a fire in the stove and stay out here on cold afternoons?" Sam asked.

"Not so much fun. Look at the rust, and at the parts so thin you can almost see through them. Besides, there's no pipe. I think I'll leave it there, though. It gives the place atmosphere." Meg peered in the stove door and found remains of a nest, probably a mouse's nest. "We'll just keep the door closed," she said, slamming it shut.

"Look at how funny these nails are," Sam said, ready to sweep them into a trash bag.

"Save them. Dad says they're handmade, that's why they're all a little different. Here's a box." She handed Sam a wooden box that might have held cranberries at another, long ago time. "I wish Ben were here. He could sit next to the stove and tell us stories. I don't know how those families got along without television. Doesn't it seem quiet out here?"

"Quiet, and cold. Why does it seem so much colder inside than on the outside?"

"It shouldn't. With that broken window, it should be the same temperature in here as outside. Maybe Dad can help fix that. Why don't you open the back door?"

Sam left the job of saving nails and pushed the back door as wide as it could go. Meg could see Beauty standing out in the field. She filled a trash bag with unusable junk, then looked out again. Beauty had moved closer. Meg carried the bag into the front room and set it next to the cranberry sorter.

"Well, hi," Meg said softly when she returned. Beauty answered with a nicker, her shaggy head poking in the open door. If the shed had not been several feet above the level of the field in back, Beauty might have walked right in.

"I know about curiosity and cats," Sam said, "but not about ponies. This one teaches me something new every day."

April hit the farm with a warm breeze, saving Meg from the admission that taking care of a pony in winter was not the greatest time in her life. Only Sam had made it bearable. Between them they had cleaned the tack room, made pegs out of dowels, and hung the saddle and bridle on the wall.

Lessons at High Ridge would begin on Saturday, the first day of spring vacation marking the end of winter and the beginning of a new riding season.

"My grandmother sent me a check for my birthday," Sam said, as they rode to school on Friday. Meg had not known about Sam's birthday, and it bothered her that Sam hadn't told her. After all, she told Sam just about every thought she had. "Oh, it's not until next month," Sam went on, "but Gram's always early. I've decided. I'm going to take a lesson at High Ridge and see what this horse business is all about."

"You had a whole winter when you could have ridden Beauty," Meg said.

"Me on that little thing? My legs would have worn a path in the snow. I need something big, like that Chieftain."

"Oh, Chieftain," Meg said. She sighed. "You'll wear out your running legs kicking Chieftain."

"Come with me and take a lesson, too."

Meg thought of the extra hay needed because of the bad winter, and shook her head. "I'll come and watch. You need someone to sit on the fence and cheer you on."

\*  \*  \*

Mrs. Madison and Tina stood next to the fence where Meg perched Saturday morning. Callie had led Sam to the barn. Vanessa and Nicole were already trotting in the intermediate ring, crowding other riders, and weaving in and out of traffic like sports cars.

Meg gasped when Sam rode into the beginners' ring. She was not on Chieftain, but on a taller, dark horse that moved with a steady gait. Sam looked uncomfortable among the smaller children, many of whom rode ponies of various sizes. None of the ponies had any of Beauty's elegance and that consoled Meg.

Callie rode her own large pony toward the intermediate ring, stopping long enough by the fence to whisper, "His name's Bluto. Jane got him this winter. Chieftain is now retired. Too bad Bluto wasn't here when you took lessons."

Meg felt a bit of envy as she watched Sam balance awkwardly on the big horse, who knew exactly how to behave in the ring, even if Sam didn't. But somehow Sam had got what Meg never had, and on her first lesson, too.

After the lesson, Sam met them at the car. "That was great fun. I can see why you love riding, Meg. Watching you all winter made me feel like I knew what I was doing."

Meg opened the door so Sam could get in, but Sam shook her head. "The Barn Rats have asked me to stay. They have extra sandwiches. Vanessa's mother will drive me home around three. Want to stay, Meg?"

The Barn Rats. That unholy group had never asked Meg to stay for lunch, not in a year of Saturdays. But on Sam's first day she got a horse that moved properly and an invitation to lunch.

"Come on, Sam, let's go. You can come too, Meg." Nicole pulled on Sam's arm impatiently. Callie waved from the farmhouse door, inviting Meg to come along. Mrs. Brown stood behind Callie and put out a beckoning arm.

Meg felt lower than Brad in the manure pile and as stubborn as Beauty. Why shouldn't she go? She'd wanted an invitation to lunch for a whole year, so why did she feel so torn?

"Come on, Meg. This is what you always wanted. An invitation from the Barn Rats," Sam whispered in her ear.

"I promised Mom I'd be home in time to feed Kara." Not true. Not true, Meg thought. But Kara would be glad to see her and maybe they could take a walk after lunch. Even Beauty would be glad to see her and Meg would teach her the same lessons Miss Jane had taught Sam. "Thanks anyway."

"I don't understand." A bit of anger in Sam's voice made Meg even more miserable.

"I don't, either," Meg mumbled.

Betty Madison put her head out the car window. "I'm a little bewildered myself. How are you going to get home?"

Sam looked uncomfortable, as if she wished she hadn't started all this. "Vanessa said her mother would drive me."

"I wish you'd told me this before," Sam's mother said. "While it was interesting watching you ride, Sam, we could have left after a little while and I could have done some grocery shopping."

Sam turned away and walked slowly toward the Brown farmhouse. She definitely didn't have her easy, carefree stride.

Meg sat quietly next to Tina and watched out the window at the blurring landscape. She should have tagged along with Sam, but she didn't want to tag after anyone. She wanted a straight invitation for herself. Sam should have known that staying with the Barn Rats would hurt her feelings. A rush of anger at her best friend dried up her tears. How could Sam betray her?

Later, in the field, Meg leaned forward until her face touched Beauty's mane. Meg could feel the comforting pulse of the pony's neck. "You and me. That's all we need. We have each other." In the ring Meg straightened up and worked Beauty on proper leads. They walked, trotted, and cantered until the softened ground showed bare spots, at last.

*   *   *

The next day, Meg walked around the farmhouse kitchen, following her mother, who chopped onions and peppers on a chopping board, then mixed a batch of muffins, while chasing Kara away from the screen door.

"I'll take Kara for a walk in a minute. I just have to talk to you first." Meg began spooning muffin batter into the tins. "Sam stayed with the Barn Rats and had lunch at the Browns'. I'm afraid I'm losing my best friend."

"Not Sam," her mother said, lifting her eyes from her cooking. "You and Sam have been together almost every day since you met."

"I know. But yesterday at High Ridge, she left me and ate with the Barn Rats."

Her mother led her to the table and sat down. "Weren't you invited?" Once in a while her mother focused directly on her, and Meg found it a little unsettling. She tried to form her thoughts.

"Yes. Sort of. Because they invited Sam, not because they wanted me."

"Oh." Her mother dropped her eyes and ran a hand through her hair. "I don't want to play Mrs. Kirtland, the teacher, but this happens all the time, and mostly to girls. Someone's in, someone's out, and the victim can't do much about it."

Meg found it easier to talk to Mrs. Kirtland than to her mother. "Sam's in, and I'm out. And I want in. And I can't lose my best friend." She hit the table with her fist.

Kara came over and hit the table with her fist, reaching up to do it. She laughed. Meg smiled at the little mimic and felt less fierce.

"Have you any idea how you can accomplish this miracle? Usually kids grow out of it. Next year you might be the most popular one. I remember a year when none of my students sat at Darlene's desk for fear of getting Darlene germs. Now she's a twirler with the band and has a whole group of girls following her."

Meg opened her fist and examined her fingers. "I thought that if the Barn Rats could spend some time over here with Sam, then it would make us all one group."

"You mean like a tea party? Something in the afternoon?"

"Mom, Barn Rats don't drink tea. They muck out stalls and clean mud out of hooves. I know they sometimes sleep in the hayloft in the summertime. If I had a sleepover here, then I could show them what a great farm this is. They could meet Beauty."

"I spend most of my year in a classroom of fourth-graders and then come home to you four. That's enough children for one person. I hate to think of more children, even if it's just for one night."

"Not so many. Callie, Sam of course, and Vanessa and Nicole."

"Those two. From all you've said, I'm surprised you want them."

Her mother got up to put the muffins in the oven, breaking up their private talk. Meg tried to be patient, even though talking to a person's back was not the same as face-to-face. "Don't you see? They're trying to take Sam away from me. I thought if they all came here, then I'd be part of the Barn Rats. Callie's really the head of the group because it's her place, but Vanessa and Nicole are the ones who let you in or kick you out."

Mom closed the book she had propped next to the stove. "All right. Wednesday night. But you plan the food, and keep them out of the house till dinner. This is spring vacation, and I need my reading time."

# 10

Even Vanessa was impressed when the Barn Rats carried sleeping bags and duffels up to Meg's room.

"Gads! My mother would kill me."

Callie turned around slowly, taking in the reds and blues. "I like it."

"That's because you still have clowns and balloons on your walls," Nicole jeered.

"I'm stuck with the baby room," Callie said placidly. "When you're number eight, things stay pretty much the same. You older ones are lucky," she said to Sam, Meg, and Vanessa.

"You are so right," Nicole said.

Meg helped each of them to find a spot for their things, having decided that everyone would sleep on the floor, including herself. Nicole arranged her sleeping bag carefully, but Meg could see the brown head of a teddy bear tucked in at the end.

She's only a kid, Meg thought, and not much

older than the boys. Going to a sleepover was pretty brave of her. Meg decided to try to like the sisters as well as she liked Sam and Callie, a challenge she would have to work on.

As Meg looked at her usually neat room with its piles of bedding on the floor, she understood a little of what her mother felt about an invasion.

"Let's go outside and I'll show you Meadowbrook Farm," she said.

Sam followed closely behind her on the stairs. "Why did you do this?" she whispered in Meg's ear.

"I figured if the Barn Rats were going to adopt you, I had to get them on my side."

"You're crazy. Lunch with them was fun, and so was riding, but I only got one check from Gram, and that's gone. I can't afford too much of this horse business."

"Oh. You should have said that sooner." Meg herded everyone into the kitchen.

"Welcome," her mother said, handing out cookies like handing out report cards. "Need some help, Meg?"

Meg took a freshly baked cookie, thinking it was only on vacations that her mother had time to herself. She hoped she hadn't ruined her mother's reading with this stupid overnight. "I'll just show them the barn and the shed and introduce them to Beauty. I don't think I can mess that up.

Thanks, Mom. I won't forget this."

She took them through the shed and showed them the tack room. "You should see ours," Vanessa said after a brief look. "The walls are covered with ribbons, and we have tons of trophies."

Sam glared at her, and Vanessa softened her comment. "Of course, this is very nice."

Meg felt that "very nice" was not very nice, after all the work she and Sam had put into it. She led them out the front door to inspect the barn before she showed off Beauty. Vanessa seemed to be missing something, like manners.

"What a ruin this is. Someone ought to bulldoze it down." Vanessa guided her sister out quickly, as if worried she might stub a toe or something.

Callie tried to cover up their behavior. "Look at the size of this place. High Ridge sure could use the room. Think of all the horses you could put in here."

"The floor's not in shape for that," Meg said. "I just picture old Daisy and Blossom getting milked in here."

"I still think it would make a wonderful house," Sam said.

Beauty waited at the gate, still wearing her winter coat.

"Hey, runt," Vanessa greeted her.

Beauty ignored her and nickered to Meg, nosing in her pocket for a carrot. Meg was glad that

Beauty showed how friendly and gentle she was, but wished the pony would kick up her heels and run to the farthest corner of the field. She did not trust the sisters. Beauty ground the carrot noisily between even rows of teeth and, visitors or no visitors, waited for the saddle and bridle.

Beauty's calmness contrasted with Nicole's energy. The younger sister climbed the fence, slid over into the field, and yelled, "Saddle her up. I'll teach this runt a thing or two."

Meg clutched the gate. Suddenly it was not so important to be a Barn Rat, even if it meant losing Sam. "I rode her this morning. She doesn't want to be ridden twice."

Now Vanessa climbed the gate. "No stalling. We want to see what this runt can do."

Sam spoke up. "Meg told you no. That's all there is to it."

"Who are you, her mother?" Nicole was a pesky horsefly that never gave up.

"I'm too big for Beauty," Sam said. "I think Vanessa and Callie are, too. Meg is the only one the right size to ride the pony."

"Well, I'm smaller than Meg, and I'm a guest. Mother says guests are always right."

Meg gave up. Nicole would clamor all night if she didn't have her own way. "All right. But I'll lead her around the ring. I don't want you trying any rodeo stunts with her."

Nicole shrugged and smiled an "I'll show you" smile. Meg brought out the tack, clumsily exchanging halter for bridle. She was angry at herself for bringing this on. There was no reason why she had to be a Barn Rat. Not when she had Beauty in the field. Angrily she put on the saddle.

"I haven't seen western stuff since we went to that 4-H meeting," Vanessa said with a sniff. "But I'm sure it costs less than English gear."

"This is as easy as getting on a bicycle," Nicole said as she swung her leg over. "Lead on." She sat docilely while Meg led the pony out to the training ring. Holding on to the bridle, Meg walked slowly around the circle. She relaxed when Nicole showed no signs of foolishness, and felt they were home free when they reached the end of the circle.

Suddenly Nicole snapped herself upright and clipped Beauty with her heel, sending her from a walk into a canter and freeing the pony from Meg's grip. Both Vanessa and Nicole jumped horses recklessly, and more than once Miss Jane had yelled at them for taking desperate chances. Meg felt sick. If Beauty carried a foal, that kick might have hurt it.

Meg ran after them. Seeing Nicole head for a clump of bushes, she cut across the field and grabbed the bridle just as Nicole gathered herself for the jump. Meg pulled the pony to a stop. Nicole continued on, landing in the bushes she had planned to jump. She lay there, screaming angrily.

Meg walked Beauty back to the gate, soothing words coming through her chattering lips. She gently slid the bridle off and replaced the halter before she looked back. Nicole still shouted from the bushes, so she couldn't be too badly hurt. Meg took off Beauty's saddle and walked her down to the stream, still talking softly, assuring her everything was all right. "If you're going to have a baby, it will be just fine. Just fine." She led Beauty through the spinney, and over to the stone wall where she'd seen the rabbit that day. She tried to pretend it was any ordinary day, just she and the pony in the field, but Nicole's shouting reminded her that it wasn't just any old day.

Meg left Beauty and dragged her feet back to the accident scene. Sam and Callie had raised Nicole, and the three walked to the gate. "Nothing broken. No harm done," Sam said to Meg.

No harm done? Nicole's eyes, reddened from her crying, scared Meg. "You ought to be shot. No one stops a horse that's set for a jump."

"You do if the jump is not allowed," Meg said. "You do if some nitwit is going to ruin your pony."

"Ruin? That . . . that runt? My sister's a better jumper than you'll ever be." Vanessa was going to be just as much fun as her sister on the sleepover. Meg saw the evening stretching on till high school.

Dinner was most uncomfortable. The Barn Rats squeezed in around the kitchen table, with Meg's father on one end and her mother on the other. Brad and Dan jockeyed for places where their elbows would not be next to girls. Dan lost. He sat next to Nicole. When she snuffled to remind them how injured she was, Dan burped. Vanessa's every action told Meg that food at the Kirtland house did not measure up to Lavoie food. Only Sam and Callie ate well.

Meg had chosen hamburgers and baked beans for the meal that would make her a Barn Rat. Brad picked that meal to make the joke about the people in Boston who lived on beans, and the people in Long Island who lived on the sound. Kara, who had to sit in a high chair she'd outgrown, acted like a baby and smeared beans all over her face and the tray of her chair. Her father broke his own rule against reading at the table and hid behind the sports page. Meg wished it were tomorrow and the Barn Rats had been exterminated.

Sam, Meg, and Callie helped with the dishes while Vanessa and Nicole sulked at the table. Meg tried to make a game of doing the dishes, but even

Sam did not enter into the fun, and Callie was as exciting as mayonnaise. Dishes could not last forever, and there were the stormy sisters still sitting there. *Tomorrow, come*, Meg pleaded silently.

Kara went to bed, the boys were sent to their room, and Meg's parents grabbed books and barricaded themselves in their bedroom. Except for Nicole's sniffles, the kitchen was deadly silent. The girls played two dragging games of crazy eights before Nicole whined, "I'm tired."

Meg picked up the cards and pulled the light string. She felt a moment of joy as they climbed the dark stairs. Tomorrow was almost here.

"I never was in a house that didn't have light switches," Vanessa complained. "You must be very poor."

"Our house has no switches, either," Sam said. Sam kept on helping, even when the cause was hopeless.

"Same here," Callie added.

Once in her room, Meg pulled the overhead string so light bounced from the red and blue walls. "I like old houses," Meg said stoutly. "There's so much more room."

"We have switches, much more room than you have, and we have a swimming pool," Nicole said.

*Oh, tomorrow, please come*, Meg whispered inside her head. *Barn Rats are rodents*. When everyone was settled in their sleeping bags on the floor, she pulled the string. The room was dark and silent. Despite the hard floor, Meg found herself drifting into a sleep that would bring the morning faster.

"My back hurts." It was Nicole.

Meg reached for the string. "You can sleep in my bed."

Vanessa sat up quickly. "Not fair. This floor is harder than our floor at home. I'm not sleeping on a hard floor if Nicole sleeps in your bed."

Heat rushed to Meg's face. "Go ahead, the two of you. You can both sleep in my bed." Now everyone was sitting up, and the night she'd hoped would slip quietly away threatened to drag along, minute by minute.

"You can't sleep with me. You kick." Nicole screwed up her face until she squeezed out a few tears. "I want to go home. I want my mother."

"You are a pain," Sam said. "Go to sleep. You'll see your mother in the morning."

Vanessa stood and rolled up her sleeping bag. "Who do you think you're picking on? She's only a little kid." Now Nicole was up and gathering her things.

The overhead light made Meg's head ache. "You'll have to ask my father if he'll drive you. And he doesn't like to be woken up."

But the girls were already on the stairs, dragging their sleeping bags behind them. The sound of Nicole pounding on her parents' door woke Meg completely, and she hurtled down the stairs.

"I want to go home," Nicole wailed. Kara let out an answering wail from her room upstairs, and the door to the boys' room opened. Now everyone was awake.

"Nonsense," her mother said, her hair standing in little spikes. "It's almost midnight. Your parents will be asleep."

"My mother never sleeps," Vanessa said. "She only catnaps in case we wake up. I bet she sits up all night because we're not there."

"Well, we're not going to bother her. You can call her in the morning. I'll set you up in the living room." Her mother came out of her room and shut the door softly behind her. "Get a large, flat sheet, Meg. I'll pull out the sleeper. Sam, you get your sleeping bag and bring Meg's, too."

Her mother pulled out the queen-sized sofa bed and spread the sheet on it. "You can sleep crossways in your sleeping bags."

They tucked Nicole in the small end between the arms of the sofa, then wriggled into their sleeping bags. "That should be more comfortable than the floor," Meg's mother said. "I'll leave the hall light on as a nightlight." She threw them a kiss, and left.

Meg was between Vanessa and Callie. Sam

117

slept at the foot. Gradually the wriggling stopped as each found a space and settled in.

When Nicole screamed, it took Meg a moment to realize where she was and why she could not jump up. Still in the sleeping bag, she sort of swam across to the light.

"Something's dropping on me," Nicole cried, pointing to the ceiling. A brown eye looked down on them through a hole.

Meg's father's slippers slapped on the floor as he entered the room, and Nicole stopped her noise for a minute before beginning again. "There's someone up there."

Bill Kirtland looked up, but the brown eye had disappeared. "Brad. Come down here." He used his football voice, which could call a whole team to attention.

Brad and Dan raced barefooted down the stairs while Kara shook her crib and demanded to get out.

"What is going on?" Meg's father demanded.

Brad tried to look repentant, but a smile sneaked out. "Some lousy girl woke me up, and then I heard all this noise in the living room. So I took this . . ." he showed them a brace and bit, "and drilled a hole in the floor to see what was going on."

Meg's father did not look pleased. "Whatever

gave you the idea you could drill a hole in the floor?"

"You never said I couldn't."

"That's what I felt. Sawdust. The bed's full of it." Nicole shook out her sleeping bag and folded it. "I'm going home."

"Me, too," Vanessa said. "I don't like being spied on."

Callie shrugged. "Guess if they're going, I'm going, too."

Meg looked at Sam.

"I don't want to hurt your feelings, but I want my own bed."

Meg sat forlornly as the party broke up. Her father pulled trousers over his pajamas and put on a warm jacket before he started the van. The sleepy party trooped out.

Meg waited until the red lights turned the corner before following the boys up the stairs. "Sorry, Mom," she said as she passed the bedroom door.

"Never again." The words sounded as if they came from someone in pain.

"Never, never again," Meg vowed. If Sam preferred the Barn Rats to her, she could have them, Meg decided. At least she had Beauty in the field, and Beauty might have a foal. Comforted, Meg dropped off to sleep in her own bed.

# 11

Thursday morning of vacation dawned cloudy, inside and out. Bill Kirtland had baseball practice on the high school field, but before he left he interrupted the boys' breakfast to line them up in the kitchen. "See this?" he asked, raising the offending brace and bit. The boys nodded. "It goes up here." He reached up and opened a cabinet high above the stove. He was the only one who could reach that cabinet, and used it for things the Kirtland children were forbidden to touch. He added the brace and bit to a bow-and-arrow set already stowed there. "Not to be touched by anyone," he said sternly as he closed the door.

Dan giggled. "You're a little late." Brad hissed at him to keep quiet, but Dan plunged on. "We have a peephole so we can see who's coming up the stairs, another one to spy on Kara, and now we can check out the living room whenever we want."

120

"Traitor." Brad threatened to coat Dan with the peanut butter he had been putting on his toast, but their father lifted Brad almost to the ceiling and talked to him while the spoonful of peanut butter waved in empty air.

"You are not to make any more holes. Is that clear?"

Brad nodded. He was slowly returned to the kitchen floor.

"I think after I come back from practice, we three will take a tour of the farm and decide what else you can't do. Stick around this morning and give your mother a hand until I come back."

The boys settled down.

Why couldn't her father have done that to Nicole, Meg wondered. That girl needed a firm hand, and her father's hand was firmer than most. Meg had a hollow space inside that not even a doughnut could fill. If last night had been bad, the rest of the school year would be torment.

"Bill, what should I do about all those holes?" Janet Kirtland asked. "I know this house wasn't perfect to begin with, but I'd like to preserve what's left."

Meg's father was not worried. "Leave them, Janet. When the boys are sent to their room, they'll have something to keep them busy. They can watch Kara's room, the living room, and the stairs." He turned to Meg. "What set off that

121

nasty little girl yesterday? If I were her parent I would not have been happy to see her come home after midnight."

Meg looked at her sneakers. It was time to get some new ones, she thought.

"Meg?"

"She fell off Beauty."

"Beauty? Sweet, gentle Beauty? I can't picture her as a bucking bronco."

"Oh, it wasn't Beauty's fault. It was mine. Nicole was going to jump Beauty over a bush and I stopped her. That made her fall."

Her father hadn't been very upset about the holes in the boys' bedroom, but he definitely looked worried now. "I don't know that girl or her parents, but if they're like Nicole, they may give us some grief. I don't want anyone riding that pony except you."

Meg sat down. "You don't know Nicole, Dad. Whatever she wants to do she goes ahead and does. I've never jumped Beauty, and now with maybe a foal inside her I didn't know what would happen."

Her mother put her arm around Meg. "Why don't you just stick with Sam and forget those High Ridge girls?"

"Sam's the problem. I told you the Barn Rats like her and they don't like me. I thought if I had them over, then we could all be friends." Her voice dwindled away. After yesterday she had absolutely no chance of ever becoming a Barn Rat.

"I think your little plan backfired," her father said. "Well, keep your fingers crossed. Maybe those Lavoies are so used to Nicole having fits, they won't get upset." He lifted Meg's chin with his finger. "And don't you get upset, either. That certainly was some night." Yawning, he left for baseball practice.

Meg went out to the field to ride Beauty, who seemed unconcerned that she had thrown a Barn Rat. They took a leisurely walk around in the soft, April air. Meg searched for signs of things growing and changing, like the green spikes of iris in the stream, and the swelling crab apple buds. She reached back and patted Beauty's flank. Beauty did seem to be putting on some weight. If so, it was good that she'd stopped Nicole from jumping, regardless of what the Barn Rats thought of her.

The next four days Meg spent most of her time with Beauty, who seemed content to stay in the field. Sam didn't show up. Several times in the evenings Meg reached for the phone, but changed her mind. It was Sam's move to call after deserting with the rest of the rats. Out in the field Meg could not hear the phone ring. When she came in she checked to see if anyone had called, but no one had except for parents asking her father about the baseball schedule.

*   *   *

"It's really all your fault," Meg whispered in Beauty's ear on Monday morning. "If I hadn't been so worried about you, I wouldn't be in this fix. Don't do anything foolish now like getting out of the field. You need your rest if you're going to be a mother."

Meg would have stayed in the field and skipped school, avoiding the Lavoie sisters forever, but being the daughter of two schoolteachers, she knew playing hooky was against the law. Reluctantly she turned from the gate. Everyone else had gone. Maybe she could miss the bus. It would take an hour to walk to school, but if she dawdled she would get there after the first recess. Then she would miss being tormented by the sisters, or even worse, being snubbed by Sam.

Meg dragged her feet down Elm Street, shuffled by Sam's house, and looked up only when she reached the bus corner. Sam stood there.

"Hurry up. The buses are running late, or else you would have missed your ride," Sam said in her usual, normal, friendly way. Meg felt cheered.

"How've you been?" she asked shyly. She hadn't talked to anyone except Beauty or the family since That Night, and it was like learning to speak all over again.

"I took Thursday off to rest after your party.

124

Then I went over to muck out stalls with Callie. She's not bad, you know. That was Friday. Then we spent the weekend in Maine with my grandmother."

Meg felt as if she'd been kicked in the stomach. Sam had gone to High Ridge and hadn't even called her. Kids who cleaned out stalls became Barn Rats. She was losing Sam for sure.

The bus ride was silent, the two best friends sitting next to each other and not talking. When they climbed the school steps, Sam said, "You could come with me sometime, you know. I just figured you were busy with Beauty."

"I was," Meg said. "Very, very busy."

The morning turned out to be a disaster. Meg's mind was so busy thinking about losing Sam, she took a reading comprehension test and failed it. Worse than that, she dreaded recess, which came after math. The clock hands kept moving toward recess. Math had never been Meg's favorite subject, but now she wished the class would go on forever. Fractions and decimals became fascinating. She bent over her work so she couldn't see the sneer on Vanessa's face.

The recess bell rang. Meg dropped her book and picked it up again. Slowly she rearranged the inside of her desk to make room for the book. In the coatroom she found she could not remember which jacket she'd worn.

"Come on, slowpoke," Sam said. "My legs need a workout after all this sitting."

Meg allowed herself to be led outside, feeling as Beauty must when she would rather run away. Sam broke into a run with Meg trotting beside her. It seemed like the old times when there was no question about Sam being her best friend. The Lavoies usually jumped rope, so Meg pushed thoughts of High Ridge and the Barn Rats out of her mind. Sam was free to go to High Ridge if she wanted to. It was enough just to run together, sometimes. When they reached the soccer field, Meg turned and saw a human chain thundering after them.

"There she is, the one who almost made me break my back," Nicole shouted.

Vanessa added, "My mother was not very happy, being woken up in the middle of the night. She says it'll be a cold day in July before she lets us go over to your house again."

The sisters had corralled a long chain of girls from several classes and flew them along like the skaters' Crack-the-Whip. Meg stood still, as if she had been waiting since Wednesday for this showdown. She asked loudly, "What's bothering you?"

Nicole danced with fury. "Tell everyone why you stopped your runt and made me fall."

Sam's smooth, cool hand enclosed Meg's. It said, *Don't get into a fight. Let it be.*

Meg had no intention of fighting with Nicole. She focused on that sharp nose and remembered the teddy bear in the sleeping bag. She was just a little kid. No one was all bad, Meg told herself. But she didn't believe a word of it.

"Poor Meg," Vanessa taunted. "She's afraid to let anyone ride her runt, especially a good rider like my sister."

"Come on," Sam said, pulling on Meg's hand. "Let's go in."

But the Lavoies pressed against them. "Not until you say you're sorry," Nicole said.

Sam tried to pull Meg through the line that curved around them. The line held, pushing them backward.

"I'm not sorry," Meg said, her nose against Nicole's. "You were getting ready to jump Beauty and I had to stop you. So I did." She almost added the final touch of sticking out her tongue, but clamped her teeth to hold it back.

Vanessa wound the line tighter, jeering as she did so. "You live in a falling-down house with a field full of junk. No light switches. A poor little horse too weak to carry my sister. Poor, poor, poor."

"There's nothing wrong with Beauty. She's a pony, not a horse."

"A poor pony. A weak pony."

The word "poor" got to Meg more than "runt"

or "weak." "Poor" attacked her mother and father. Even her brothers and Kara. The line wound around her was a line of girls she went to school with. How could the sisters change them from friends to a mean gang?

Nicole danced up and down, picking up her sister's chant. "Poor, poor, poor."

"Beauty's going to have a foal."

Sam dropped Meg's hand. Nicole stopped dancing.

"A foal?" Sam asked, wonder in her voice. Meg wasn't sure Sam knew what a foal was.

"A baby. Beauty's going to have a baby." There. It was said. Meg felt sick. If Beauty did not have a foal, Meg might as well move to another town.

The bell shrilled the end of recess, shattering the line, releasing Meg and Sam.

"Why didn't you tell me?" Sam whispered as they crossed the field.

"Because it might not be true," Meg whispered back.

"Oh."

When Meg came in from the field that afternoon, she found her mother sitting at the picnic table sipping coffee from a mug. Across from her was a familiar woman. It wasn't until she looked up that Meg knew who it was. Mrs. Brown from High Ridge. Callie's mother, as well as the mother of seven others including Miss Jane. Imagine Mrs. Brown sitting in their kitchen! How often Meg had wished her mother would become a horse mother and get friendly with Mrs. Brown. Now maybe it was happening.

"Mrs. Brown heard from Callie that Beauty was going to have a foal," her mother said calmly.

Meg's face grew hot. "I didn't mean to tell. It sort of came out by itself."

Mrs. Brown smiled, pushing neat, leathery wrinkles up to her graying hair. "I feel partly responsible for your troubles. I don't have much control over those Barn Rats, except Callie, of course. Unfortunately, we need their help in the stables, or I'd send them all packing. I'm sure they pressured you, Meg."

Meg hung her head. "I'm sorry. I wasn't supposed to tell."

Her mother spoke to Mrs. Brown. "It's just that I don't know the first thing about horses. I didn't want Meg telling that Beauty was if she wasn't."

Mrs. Brown raised her mug with both hands and sniffed in the steam. "Callie also told me what happened the other night when she came home so late. Then I had a long talk with Mrs. Lavoie. She can become quite emotional. Hysterical is more like it. Your husband mustn't have been too happy about his midnight ride." She smiled again and Meg found herself smiling, too.

"He wasn't. It's too bad the girls didn't get along too well," Mrs. Kirtland said.

Mrs. Brown placed her mug firmly on the table. "Those girls are much too reckless and I threatened to bar them from High Ridge if they continued to misuse the horses. That Nicole needs firm discipline. Unfortunately, her mother spends more time playing bridge and going to parties than she does with the girls. Vanessa has become very protective of Nicole, sort of taking her mother's place. Nicole is a spoiled little girl." Mrs. Brown rubbed her hands together as if she wanted to swat Nicole on her riding seat, then looked at Meg. "About that foal . . ."

"Can you tell?"

"I'm no vet, but I'd love to take a look."

Meg heard those words and ran for her coat.

Beauty whinnied as she trotted up to the gate. Mrs. Brown laughed out loud. "No offense, Meg, but that is the funniest creature I've seen in a long time."

Meg decided she couldn't be angry at everyone. "It's shedding time. In another month she'll look like herself again."

Beauty resembled an old-fashioned quilt. Where patches of long hair had come out, the sleek, darker coat of summer shone through. Mrs. Brown managed to squeeze through the bars of the gate and slowly approached the pony. Beauty nickered for Meg, but allowed Mrs. Brown's hand to feel her belly.

"Ponies are so different from horses. It's hard to tell." She laid her head against the round stomach. "Some gurgling is going on in there, but I can't feel a leg."

Beauty nuzzled Mrs. Brown's neck. "I take that back about her being funny-looking. She's a sweet, gentle animal. I wouldn't mind having her at High Ridge for the smaller students to ride."

It was good that Mrs. Brown had her head down, working her way back through the bars of the gate. Taking care of Beauty was not the fantasy Meg had dreamed, but the idea of trucking her off to High Ridge, where smaller versions of Vanessa and Nicole would sit on her back, was too much, and Meg was sure horror showed on her face.

Mrs. Brown finally emerged through the bars. "Good for the figure. Should do this more often." She strode toward her truck and climbed in.

"I think it's best you call in a vet. It's wise to have one at the birth. All kinds of things can go wrong, my dear. I don't mean to scare you, but there are shots that must be given to ward off infection. The minute Beauty seems restless, you should call a doctor."

How can people who don't want to scare a person manage to do exactly that, Meg thought. Terror gripped her heart, replacing the day's anger. She felt battered, worn out.

"Don't let her worry you," her mother said after the truck had gone. "Beauty is healthy and has lived through a winter outside. Besides, the wedding might not have taken at all. Mrs. Brown certainly couldn't tell. I'll call Mr. Arsenius and see how he feels about a vet."

Meg went in to read one of her horse books in which everyone knew what to do and the animal caused no trouble at all.

# 12

Meg dreaded the playground, but there was no Crack-the-Whip line following her the next day. Vanessa and Nicole stood alone by the school door, and the other girls were back to their usual games.

"What do you think happened?" Meg asked Sam as they loped around the soccer field. "I tried to stay out sick today, but didn't have the nerve. I guess I'd rather face the sisters than play hooky and face my parents."

"It was that foal," Sam said. "The other girls weren't too happy with Nicole when they found out you were trying to protect a baby pony."

"I can guess what'll happen to me if there is no foal." Meg sank on a rock and ran her fingers over its rough surface.

"Cheer up. Foals don't get born in a day. School is only a few more weeks. By fall no one will remember."

True, Meg thought. Kara had taken a long time to be born, and ponies were bigger. They must take longer. She felt relieved.

Callie came across the field, smiling in a friendly way. "Mind if I sit with you? Sorry about yesterday. That Nicole ought to be spanked."

"Just about what your mother said."

"She told me. She thinks Beauty is a wonderful pony. Can I come over some day to see her?"

"Sure," Meg felt as proud as if she were an official Barn Rat.

"I told Vanessa about Mother's visit to your house and now her nose is out of joint."

"That explains why they're sulking by the door," Sam said. "Has your mother ever visited the Lavoies?"

"Good grief. No. She doesn't like silly women or whiny kids."

Sam grinned. "I think the sisters are jealous, Meg. Better watch out. They may just want you for a friend."

A warm feeling spread through Meg. Someone was jealous of her. That had never happened before. "Come over sometime, Callie. Sam and I have a great time in the field, and you could give me some tips on training Beauty."

The bell signaled the end of recess and Callie, Meg, and Sam linked arms. At the door, Meg broke the chain. She had only seen the Lavoies at their snootiest, arming their words with barbs, or upsetting the riders in the ring. This was the first time she'd seen them standing alone, and she thought of her resolve to find something nice about them. Nicole was a baby who needed a teddy bear, and Vanessa at least was loyal to her sister. Those were the only nice things she could think of, so she guessed they'd have to do for now.

"How's your back, Nicole?" Meg managed to be polite.

Nicole groaned dramatically and grabbed her back to show she was still in great pain.

Meg stepped lightly into the hall and caught up with Sam.

Everyone was in the field Saturday morning; Meg's father out to check on the pony, the boys to look for something to tear down, Meg's mother, Kara, and Sam and Meg.

"She looks just the way she did when she came," her father said. "Except, of course, for that coat."

Sam and Meg pulled handfuls of winter hair off, dropping it on the ground for birds to use as nesting material. Patches of hair lazily moved on a spring wind like dandelion fluff. "We work on it every day, but it's going to take forever. I don't know how Mr. Arsenius had her so beautiful last July."

"She was beautiful because I had two boys helping me, and a whole family to do the grooming." Mr. Arsenius appeared at the gate.

Meg's heart leaped. At last her questions would be answered, and all her worries quieted. She just hoped he wouldn't tell her there was no foal.

"Come join the crowd," her father said. "I have a few minutes before baseball practice. These girls have been concerned."

As if he hadn't, Meg thought. She and Sam stepped back and clapped the curry combs against the shed. Mom held Kara tightly, not ready to let her run around the hooves, but Kara was happy with a fistful of mane in one hand, and a bunch of Beauty's winter coat in the other. Brad and Dan sidled up, closer than they usually dared to get to the pony.

"You have boys helping you?" Brad asked.

"I had to hire two to help me with my growing herd," Mr. Arsenius said. "The boys keep the fences, feed and water, and take care of the stallion."

Brad's eyes rounded with wonder. He was not too fond of horses, but the thought of earning money doing outside work obviously appealed to him. "Can we work for you?"

Mr. Arsenius laughed, his small mustache spreading thinly as his mouth widened. "Get experience here. Help your dad with the fences.

Learn how to groom. When you're older, we'll see."

Meg watched Mr. Arsenius's deft hands feel all over the pony. "You've done a good job," he said to her. "I see she finally let herself get caught."

Meg's face grew hot. "That was a long time ago."

"Well, I'm no vet, but then we've needed one only a few times, mostly for small cuts and infections. We let our mares roam the hill behind our place, and they bring their foals out to meet us when they're ready."

He felt around Beauty's belly again. "She's so solidly packed, I can't feel anything extra. Sometimes you can feel a leg, but I feel nothing."

Despair. Beauty's foal became more important every day.

"These little beasts can surprise you, though, so don't give up hope. Just set your mind on her having a filly."

"A filly?"

"Little girl pony. Colts are male and much harder to handle, whereas fillies are easy from the beginning."

Meg kept her eyes down so she wouldn't let the boys know she often felt the same way.

"You do any riding, Mrs. Kirtland?" Mr. Arsenius asked.

137

She shook her head. "I was going to last fall, but I'm too big for Beauty. I don't have time, anyway."

"You've got room in this field. You should have a horse. Then Meg could move on to it when she's older. This little one here should be able to ride Beauty or the foal, if there is one." He patted Kara's head.

Meg's mother shook her head. "Don't put ideas in their heads. We are not a horsey family, and we're certainly not rich. Meg's got her dream, which was my dream once, and that's enough for us."

Meg's father plucked a wad of Beauty's winter coat off his T-shirt. "I've got to get going. You're sure there's no need for us to do anything about the pony?"

"Not a worry in the world. We stand behind our Shetlands."

"Not too close," Brad said. He escaped the laughter by running up the driveway to watch the Sky Farm truck drive off.

Meg scratched big X's on her wall calendar. Only six school days remained uncrossed.

Robins and catbirds sang a joyous symphony at four in the morning, starting so abruptly that Meg imagined a knob turned suddenly to *on*. She listened drowsily for a minute and then leaped out of bed. Today might be the day.

Fumbling fingers pulled on blue pants and a blue-and-white checkered shirt. Meg dragged a comb once through her tangled hair. She was crazy, crazy, crazy, she chanted to herself as she ran lightly down the stairs. There was no proof that Beauty was carrying a foal, not from Mrs. Brown and not from Mr. Arsenius. So why was she so certain that today would be the day, or that there would be any special day at all?

She slathered peanut butter thickly on a piece of bread, then stuck a banana in her pocket. She went out through the shed, where tack hung neatly on hooks and the wavy old glass winked at her as she passed. Her father had replaced the missing pane with newer glass, and hung up some of his sports ribbons to make the tack room look more authentic.

Meg felt so certain today was the day, she even considered inviting all the Barn Rats over to prove that Beauty had a foal.

She closed the shed door. Breath caught in her throat. No Beauty nickered a welcome. The world was pale gray, alive with noise. A chipmunk chittered convulsively, a catbird sang in the crab apple tree, but there was no whinny, no nicker, no throb of hooves.

Was there a movement beneath the pink blizzard of apple blossoms? Did a tail swish among the blue flag iris? Meg looked and listened, but did not call for Beauty. She felt the way she did when she waited for something to come in the mail. Imagining a letter curled in the mailbox was more satisfying than finding the box empty and having to wait another day.

The sun poked up, a round, red ball promising June heat. A shrill whinny from the thicket greeted it.

"Beauty?" Wind whispered in her ear. Perhaps she had been mistaken.

Beauty emerged from the thicket and moved along the stone wall at the north end of the field. She walked slowly away from Meg, stopping here and there to crop. Meg fixed her gaze on the pony until her eyes watered from the strain. The pony in her sleek summer coat shimmered and blurred.

"Here, Beauty. Come here." Beauty took another step away just as she had last summer. This was so unlike the usual morning dash to the gate with a welcoming nicker that Meg felt she had lost a friend. She squinted. Was something moving between the pony and the stone wall? Meg took a step and again a shadow seemed to step with Beauty.

"Meg. You've got to get ready for school."

"Mom, come here. I think it's come. Please help me look."

Her mother squeezed through the gate and carried Kara above the dewy grass. Brad and Dan followed, shoving each other and rattling their lunch boxes.

"It's not like her to stay by the wall. When I call she usually comes running."

Dan pulled his brother's arm. "Come on, Brad, we'll run over and get the scoop."

Mom barred them with her free arm. "Oh, no you won't, young man. All three of you are off this minute for the bus. If there's anything with Beauty it will still be there this afternoon."

"Go to school?" Meg asked. "Mrs. Brown said all kinds of things could happen. Beauty might need a shot."

"You heard Mr. Arsenius. There's nothing to worry about. High Ridge only has horses, and ponies are different. What Beauty needs is time for herself. And quiet. As a mother, I know that. Now, go."

Meg forced one foot in front of the other down the road to the bus stop.

"Probably nothing there," Dan said, running rings around her. "Just your imagination."

"But she's full of hot air, just like Dan." Brad ran ahead.

Meg was going to keep the whole thing secret, but the secret lasted one full minute when Sam joined her. "Please, please don't tell anyone else. You know Nicole. She'll be over to try to jump the baby this afternoon."

Sam crossed her heart solemnly. "You'd better keep your eyes closed today. They shine so much the sisters will guess your secret."

Meg practiced on the bus, but there were so many exciting pictures behind her eyes, she gave up. All day she kept her eyes on books she didn't read and papers she didn't finish. She walked around the playground she didn't see and ate a lunch that had no taste. It would be a lie if she crossed this school day off her calendar because she hadn't really been to school at all. She had left her mind in the field.

Meg wriggled on the bus seat that afternoon, certain she could run faster than the bus moved. There had to be something special out there in the field to have kept Beauty from greeting her that morning.

"I can't stand this," Sam said. "You want my seat, too? Then you'll have more room to wiggle in."

"No." She took a deep breath and put her hands in her lap. "See? I'm calm." Her hands leapt up and began twisting each other. "Well, not really. But I've never had a baby before."

Sam laughed. "One more corner and we're at Elm Street. Mind if I come straight home with you?"

"You have to," Meg said. She pulled herself up and stood by the bus door, holding on as the bus turned the corner.

The doors folded aside, and Meg leaped, skipping the steps entirely. "Come on," she urged, as Sam took the steps, one at a time. "Don't you dare get ahead of me, though. It's my pony, so I should see it first."

Sam matched Meg's pace as they walked up Elm Street. Leaves hid the field so there was no chance of getting a first peek. As they crossed the stream, Meg realized there were cars parked in front of her house. It looked like the whole volunteer fire department had been called out.

Meg began to run, Sam still at her side. Her mother waved from the fence, holding Kara on the gate with her other hand. Mrs. Brown and Callie stood beside her. "After you left for school, I felt I had to tell someone. I just called a few people. Betty, and Mrs. Brown, and your father. I don't know how the others found out," her mother said sheepishly.

Her father had come home early and was talking

to Betty Madison. Several mothers of High Ridge students chatted while their young ones hung on the bottom rail. Meg felt a little cheated. It was her pony, not her mother's. Where were all of you people those days when I couldn't even get near Beauty? she thought. Where were you the day Beauty ran away? It seemed that everyone was interested in Beauty's foal, or maybe it was just a long time between the town's two parades, and people were ready for a little excitement.

The crowd scene got worse. The Lavoies jumped out of their station wagon, the sisters running headlong to the gate. Nicole would have gone through if Meg's father had not grabbed her and given her a little shake. Mrs. Lavoie was so busy talking to the other High Ridge mothers, she didn't even notice.

"Is it here?" Meg asked her mother.

Her mother nodded.

"What is it, a filly or a colt?"

"Beauty's keeping it way at the other side of the field. She won't let anyone see."

Smart Beauty. Beautiful Beauty.

Brad came up behind her. "I hope it's a colt and not a filly. Mr. Arsenius says colts give you more trouble."

"Then you'll have to learn how to handle it if you want to work at Sky Farm," Meg said. Brad stopped teasing.

"You're the only one she'll let near, Meg," her mother said. "Why don't you go out and see what it is?"

Meg put a handful of oats in a bucket and moved slowly out into the field. Once again she was stalking a wary pony. Beauty matched each step she took. Meg shook the bucket, the oats pinging enticingly. Beauty turned, keeping that shadow on her far side, and sauntered toward the thicket. Meg lay in a low spot and peered under Beauty. Tiny perfect legs moved double-time in rhythm with the mare. All eight legs disappeared into the thicket. Filly or colt, Beauty was not going to let anyone near it.

"I saw the legs," she shouted as she ran back to the gate.

"Smart animal. Good mother," Mrs. Brown said briskly. "Glad to see there weren't any complications."

When it became apparent that Beauty was not ready to show her foal, the crowd dwindled. Nicole and Vanessa were whisked away before they said a word, and Mrs. Brown took Callie home. Soon only Sam was left. "Come walk the field with me," Meg said. "Maybe you'll have a chance to see the legs."

They circled the field, always conscious that somewhere two pairs of eyes might be watching. Down near the flag iris at the edge of the stream, they found Beauty's distinct hoofprints, with the tiniest perfectly formed indentations the foal had left beside them. Meg wished she had a footprint kit to preserve the marks of those tiny hooves.

"It's no use," Meg said, "she's not going to let us see it until she's ready. I'm so tired from all this excitement I've got to go in."

Sam seemed less weary, and helped Meg through the gate.

When Sam walked home, Meg went in to finish the day's schoolwork. The lost feeling of the morning still remained. The waiting was over. Now Beauty had company in the field and might never need Meg again. She sat at the kitchen table and spread out the work that she had missed. Who cared about fractions? There was a new animal who had never been in the world before, walking next to its mother. Beauty was so clever, keeping it always on her far side, always away from the visitors and from Meg. It was so hard not to be able to see the foal or to touch it.

"Wasn't this an exciting day?" her mother asked. "I could never have made those phone calls if my class hadn't had art. I hardly taught at all, just handed out work sheets. Now I have to correct them. I hope you don't mind that I called everyone. How about hamburgers for supper?"

Meg listened in amazement as her mother rattled on. It wasn't like her to talk so much. "I don't mind as long as no one else sees the foal before me. I guess Beauty's doing the same thing you did when you had Kara. You left us kids here. We couldn't see the baby until you brought her home. You got to see Kara first. I guess I'll just have to wait until Beauty brings her baby home." Meg closed her math book. "I think it's too late for me to flunk fifth grade. Anyway, fractions aren't real life."

Janet Kirtland put down the skillet and walked over to hug Meg. "Beauty's still yours, and the foal is, too. Just give them time to get to know each other."

"But Beauty may not need me anymore." Meg felt like putting her head on the table and bawling.

"Nonsense. I still need my mother. When you have children, I'll still be part of your life." The hug was more comforting than the words.

Meg picked up the pencil. "Just five more school days and then I can live in the field again. With my two ponies." She brightened a bit and reopened her book. "Hamburgers sound great," she added.


All Friday afternoon and the whole day Saturday, Meg and Sam followed Beauty and her shadow around the field. "It's like when I first got her. She doesn't need me," Meg said.

Sam grabbed her hand and squeezed it. "Remember how she used to watch us run and then move closer when we paid her no attention? Come on. Let's get some exercise."

The girls ran around the edge of the field. Beauty kept her foal hidden and moved away from them, but she seemed to know where they were all the time.

On Sunday night, Meg and Sam sat on the gate and swatted black flies. Sam pinched one between her nails. "I hate these humpbacked critters. Seems unfair to go through a tough winter and then get chewed to death. Come to think of it, they're kind of like Nicole and Vanessa. Nasty nips and then disappear."

Meg scratched a spot of blood on her arm. "Come on, Beauty, save me from these bugs. Give me some answers to the question I'll get at school tomorrow. Hurry, before school ends and I won't have a chance to brag about your baby and tell them it's a filly or a colt."

A soft nicker behind the shed silenced her. Beauty walked around the corner and right up to Meg, making soft noises in her throat.

Beauty turned slightly to reveal the foal. Its back touched Beauty's belly, but it stood unafraid on tiny legs and perfectly formed miniature hoofs. There was a touch of red in its coat and the soft beginnings of a light mane and tail. The head was large and blunt, and the eyes seemed to focus straight ahead in human fashion. The short tail swished away the black flies.

Beauty allowed Meg to touch the foal's soft nose and then moved between them. When the mare turned, the foal turned with her and almost touched her as they walked back into the field.

Meg and Sam sat, bewitched by the magic of the moment, until Meg remembered the big question everyone had asked for the last three days. She slipped from the gate and examined the foal.

It was a filly. Meg hugged herself. "A filly," she said softly to Sam. "I'll name her," she paused in the perfect spring of that wonderful year, "Little One. But I'll register her as Meadowbrook's Trailing Arbutus."

The two friends clasped hands and watched Beauty lead Little One out into the field.

"What a year," Meg said. "I wouldn't mind being eleven all over again. Imagine, having two ponies in the field, and a best friend to enjoy them with."

"I could stand another year like this one myself," Sam said. "What excitement are you planning for sixth grade?"

Meg grinned. "I don't think I'll start wanting anything for at least a month. I'm kind of full-up right now. Did you see how Beauty just brought Little One right up to me? And I was so worried I'd be left out."

Meg slid off the gate and into the field. "Let's pick some crab apple blossoms for our moms. I know mine is waiting in the kitchen. I've got to tell her about Beauty bringing Little One right to the gate. I can't believe how excited Mom got when the foal was born. Did you ever hear of anyone getting that excited?"

Sam looked down at the ground where starry bluets burst through the greening grass. "No, Meg." Her voice trembled a little with laughter. "I never knew anyone who got that excited about a pony and her foal. Never."

## About the Author

Marion Doren is the author of *Borrowed Summer* and *Nell of Blue Harbor*. When she taught fourth grade in Southborough, Massachusetts, Scholastic books were a big part of the curriculum. But she never imagined that one day she'd write one herself. A graduate of Connecticut College, Ms. Doren is married to a musician and teacher and has four children.